Locced and Loaded Ladies: Daleigh's Journey

Locceed and Loaded Ladies, Volume 1

Candi Jones

Published by Candi Usher, 2024.

This is a work of fiction. Similarities to real people, places, or events are entirely coincidental.

LOCCED AND LOADED LADIES: DALEIGH'S JOURNEY

First edition. October 3, 2024.

Copyright © 2024 Candi Jones.

ISBN: 979-8227353801

Written by Candi Jones.

Table of Contents

Locced and Loaded Ladies: Daleigh's Journey (Locceed and Loaded Ladies, #1) 1
    Table of Content 2
    Prologue 4
    A Matted Mess 5
    Detangling 11
    The Big Chop 16
    New Growth 24
    Getting Started 29
    Twisted 36
    Locced In 42
    Growing It Out 48
    Retwist 57
    Locced and Loaded 68
    74
    76

LOCCED AND LOADED

A WOMAN'S HAIR JOURNEY AND FINDING HER TRUE SELF

By Candi Usher

Table of Content

P<u>rologue</u>
   <u>A Matted Mess</u>
<u>Detangling</u>
<u>The Big Chop</u>
<u>New Growth</u>
<u>Getting Started</u>
<u>Twisted</u>
<u>Locced In</u>
<u>Growing It Out</u>
<u>Retwist</u>
<u>Locced and Loaded</u>

Prologue

Daleigh ran when she got the chance. But was her past really behind her? She had been running from things all her life. Was she finally at the place to settle down? Had she found what she was looking for? Things look different. With the past that she packed up and left behind, she believed she was moving on. But when there was a knock on the door, it seemed her past wouldn't let her go. How will Dayleigh begin again? She could go on the run again. Disappear into the night. Yet, she didn't want to leave the life she created. Was staying worth it? Or should she leave to protect the people who had started to mean so much to her? She would discover that the life she thought existed was never real.

A Matted Mess

Daleigh walked into the hair salon with her last $50. She didn't know what she was doing, but she was doing it. She sat, waiting for her turn, and began looking at the prices, deciding what she wanted to do with her hair. It took a lot of confidence coming into the shop. She knew she needed a change after changing cities and her life.

Daleigh (pronounced Day-lee) was from Videl, a small town in Georgia. She was only 18 years old. She was a chocolate-skinned girl with unusual eyes that were an eerie shade of purple. She didn't look like either of her parents. She didn't look like anyone on either side of her family. She was 5'10" tall with legs for days. She had some curves but felt more significant than other people considered curvy. Daleigh's coiled hair was to her shoulders and purple on the ends. Her voice was firm yet soft because she felt if she spoke too loud, she would sound harsh or angry. She was an only child. She was also an all-A student in school. Her life was sheltered and wrapped tight by two domineering and overwhelming parents. They didn't care; Daleigh was trying to prove she was the perfect child for them.

Her dad, Jason Miller, was a teacher who loved to control everything and everyone. Her mom, Casey Miller, was teetering on the edge of a nervous breakdown every week. The family was in constant disarray. Daleigh's grandparents didn't even want her mother. They constantly made it clear that Daleigh wasn't welcome to family events. Her father's family intentionally cut him off. The amount of control he needed was out of control. He would ruin family functions by starting fights deliberately. He would get loud and boisterous; no alcohol was necessary. They avoided him at all costs. This means they avoided Daleigh, too. She had begged her dad and her mom's family to get her out of that house. Yet they refused to help her. Daleigh was left to fend for herself.

Daleigh was always looking for a way out of Videl after graduation. There was nothing for her there. Marcus Domingez came as a disguised blessing. She met him on her eighteenth birthday. She worked at the Waffle House. Dayleigh had worked there from sixteen until graduation. Marcus had showed up the day after graduation. He was 6'3", with mocha-colored skin and hair that was so curly you knew he was of Puerto Rican descent. He was a trucker who was supposed to be passing through. He made a point to be seated in Daleigh's section, flirting with her every chance he could. Marcus made a point to show up every day. Daleigh basked in his attention since the guys in her town had no ambition, and very few made it out. She thought Marcus was going to be her ticket out of Vadel. She was so wrong.

NEXT THING DALEIGH knew, Marcus had moved to town. He was adamant about "rescuing" her after she told him what was happening at home. He even dared to go and confront her father, which was a huge mistake. That man made such a fuss that Marcus ran out of the house. Daleigh followed, embarrassed that the neighbor had come out of their homes because of the yelling and screaming. Her father stood in the middle of the road and screamed for her to return. Her mother had a meltdown in the middle of the road. Marcus and Daleigh got in Marcus' Mustang and drove off. They passed the police coming up the road. Daleigh couldn't imagine the mess that was about to happen in the neighborhood. Unfortunately, she needed to go back and get her things. She didn't want to ever return to that house again.

Marcus took Daleigh back to his house, hoping she would stay with him permanently. He intentionally riled up her parents. He needed a way to make Dayleigh dependent on him. He was ok with her working at the Waffle House. If she stepped carefully and didn't flirt with other men, she could make her measly money.

"She's going to need me forever. I will never let her go!!" Marcus thought to himself. He looked over at Daleigh, smiling. Marcus was a man who took whatever he wanted whenever he wanted. He had intentionally moved to Vadel. When he met Daleigh, he wanted her. Trucking was a decent life, but it wasn't the life he wanted to keep doing. Driving trucks did allow Marcus to find the women he wanted, though. He always made sure to have the women hooked on him just enough so he could control them any way he could. He almost was caught playing the field a few times, but that silver tongue always got him out of it.

"I'm so sorry about my parent, Marcus," Daleigh mumbled, still embarrassed and not wanting to look Marcus in the face.

"It's ok. It's my fault for even going over there. I provoked them, and I'm sorry." Marcus stated.

"Okay." Daleigh nodded.

Marcus pulled up to his house, got out, and then walked around to open the door for Daleigh.

"Thank you," Daleigh said softly.

She and Marcus walked up to the door of Marcus' 3-bedroom house. He opens the door for her, ushering her in. Daleigh walks to the couch. She can't control the sobs that suddenly overtake her. Her life is going wild, and she feels there's nothing she can do about it. Marcus sits next to her and then wraps his arms around her. If Daleigh had looked up at that moment, she would have seen the smirk on Marcus' face. He had her right where he wanted her. Next move, then checkmate. Daleigh's face was buried too deep in his chest, and his eyes were closed, so he could not even sense the change in Marcus' body language.

"I think you should move in with me. That way, you'll be safe, and you don't have to keep dealing with the drama from your parents." Marcus suggested gently.

"Would that be a good idea? We're not married, and I wouldn't feel comfortable staying with you in that capacity." Daleigh answered.

"Just for a few days. Until you can find your place to live." Marcus prodded.

Daleigh looked into Marcus' brown eyes, her violet eyes still damp.

"OK. Sure. But only for a few days. I can apply for an apartment or find a friend to stay with. I don't want to be more of a burden to you than I already am. Thank you for caring so much about me."

"I love you. I want to see you happy. You've been through so much with your parents, and you deserve to have a happy life. I hope I can give you that. I'm always here for you. You staying here is no problem." Marcus consoled Daleigh. Marcus' mind began running again. Step one had now happened. Daleigh may have been the easiest target he had ever come across in his 36 years of life. See, he told Daleigh that he was only 20 years old. No one in town knew his age because he had purchased a fake identity. Oh, his name was real. That's the only thing in his life that was real. Marcus had done so many things in his life that if Videl knew who he was, people would lock their homes and daughters up. Marcus' past was so dark that there was no way any light could soften it.

Marcus' condescending smile broke through again as he stared at the beautiful yet unaware young woman in his arms. He was going to break her. Her parents had already done part of the job for him. He wanted her so dependent on him that she would have to ask his permission to breathe. He didn't want Daleigh's body. He wanted her soul. Marcus wanted her to become his mannequin. He enjoyed the challenge of breaking a woman into the image he wanted her in. When he was tired of her, he would leave the shell of her for someone else to deal with. The trail of broken spirits was like a high to Marcus. Every city he chose, each woman he chose, he made sure the next one was harder than the last. Daleigh may be his last one, though. She was too easy, and Marcus could easily make her his wife. He intentionally never married because he didn't want to be tied down. Marriage meant that, at some point, he could lose control. Yet, Daliegh was the clay he always craved. He was willing to take his chance on her permanently. She was unaware, and he was the snake waiting to strike his poison, filling every cell of her with him.

Daleigh finally calmed down. She went to the bathroom to clean her face and blow her nose. Something in her didn't feel right; she couldn't place her finger on it. It felt like Marcus' attitude had changed once they had settled into his house. Maybe it was the stress of the day. Daleigh thought she was overthinking things. Marcus was loving, kind, and caring and had her back when no one else did. She knew she could depend on him.

Just as Daleigh came out of the bathroom, the doorbell rang. Marcus moved quickly to the door, hoping it wasn't anything or anyone who could get in the way of his plans. Things were coming together too quickly, and that was unsettling to him. He brushed the feeling off and opened the door to two police officers standing in the doorway.

"Good evening, sir. We're here to check on Daleigh Miller. Is she here right now?" the taller White officer asked. Marcus looked the man up and down, then turned to the Hispanic female officer beside him. He flashed her his unique smile, then answered, "Yeah. She just stepped into the bathroom. Let me get her for you."

"Why are you here, officers?" asked Daleigh. "Did my parents send you here? Nothing is happening, no one is injured, and we left the altercation before it worsened. Why are you bothering us?"

"Your parents just want to make sure you're ok. Your mom had a breakdown and had to be medicated. They just transported her to the hospital. She thinks your boyfriend kidnapped you." the Hispanic officer answered.

"Well, Officer...what's your name? Diaz? I am just fine. I'll check on my mother later. If there's nothing else, please leave." Daleigh huffed, getting frustrated and stressed all over again.

"Baby, calm down. Your parents care about you and want to make sure you're ok. Don't take it the wrong way. How about this? Let's go to the hospital, check on your mom, and let her and your dad see you're okay. No drama, no mess. Just a simple pass-through." Marcus encouraged.

"Fine. Goodbye, officers!!" Daleigh shut the door in the officers' faces. She was so tired of her parents. Even though she was not in the house, they still wanted control of her life. After the hospital trip, Daleigh no longer wanted to deal with them again. It was time to cut ties with the people she felt would eventually drive her insane.

"Come on. Let's hurry up and go so we can leave sooner. I don't want to deal with my parents anymore after this. I'm tired of them attempting to control my life." Daleigh was nearly in tears again.

"Baby, it's ok.

Marcus and Daliegh went to the care. Marcus was looking forward to stirring up so much more mess. He needed to be sure Daleigh was entirely in his hands. Dayleigh was wondering what drama her parents were getting ready to stir up. She already knew that her mother being sedated was only temporary, and showing her face could get her to leave her alone for a few weeks. She felt things would be okay if her parents could trust she was safe with Marcus. Both Daleigh and Marcus smiled at the same time. Marcus' was mischievous, while Dayleigh was one of trepidation and longing.

Detangling

Marcus and Daleight arrived at the Videl Memorial Hospital in record time. Marcus was ready to set off the fireworks. He turned to Dayleigh.

"Babe. I am here for you. If you need me to, I will defend you. I know your parents don't care for me, but I love you so much, and I don't want to see you hurt by them again after what happened earlier."

Dayleigh cupped Marcus' face with her hand, stroking his jaw with her thumb.

" I know. I'm just scared because I don't know what's about to happen. My mom having to be sedated is a serious business. I don't want her to get riled up again. Earlier today was enough to make me not want to talk to her or my dad for a few days. If it hadn't been for them sending the police, I wouldn't have to go in now."

Marcus leaned over and kissed Daleigh's jaw, then exited the car. He walked around to her side and opened the door for her. She thanked him, grabbed his hand after he closed the car door, took a deep breath, and headed into the hospital.

They arrived at the front desk. Daleigh asked what room her mother was in, and they headed to the elevators. Marcus' mind began rehearsing the words he was going to say. He wanted to ensure that his words were the right knife to the heart. He felt Daleigh parents were in her business too much, and he needed them cut off so Daleigh would be entirely his. Marcus glanced over at Daliegh, knowing that she had no idea the volcano was about to erupt. He was ready to get things going and prepared to mentally and emotionally make Daleigh dependent on him.

Daleigh sighed deeply as they walked down the hall. She stopped outside of her mother's hospital room door. She looked through the small window, watching her father interact with her mother. From looking at them, you wouldn't think Casey had just had a nervous breakdown. Casey and Jason were giggling that nothing had happened that day. Daleigh opened the door quietly, Marcus not far behind her.

"Mom, Dad," Daleigh said.

"Daleigh, hi sweetheart!!" Casey said, her voice oddly extra high and excited. Daleigh could tell her mother was very drugged. Her eyes were glassy and dilated.

"Daughter," Jason said in a low and stern voice, his smile changing to a frown after he saw Marcus come in behind Daleigh.

"Mr and Mrs Miller. I hope you're feeling better, Mrs Miller." Marcus said, smiling in his head. He was gearing up for the headline.

"Why are you here, Marcus? We don't need you around. You've already caused enough trouble." Casey nearly screamed. She noticed Marcus's presence in the room after Jason had said something to him. It felt like the temperature had dropped to below freezing in the room. Casey knew it wasn't the tranquilizers because she was still feeling warm and high off of them. Marcus was killing that buzz, though.

"I'm here to ensure you don't hurt Daleigh again. I asked her to move in with me. I think she would be safe from you." Marcus smirked, going in for the kill.

"NO!!!" Casey screamed. She clapped her hands on the side of her face. "My daughter will not stay with you. You will not destroy our family!!!" Jason's face turned bright with rage.

"You will not live with him!! I will not allow you to move out of our house. You don't know him well enough. He is not safe!!" Jason raged.

"Mr Miller. Do you think she's safe with you? You slapped her earlier for arguing with you. Your wife just had another breakdown." Marcus argued back. He wrinkled his nose in disgust at the smell of alcohol, medication, and sickness the hospital room reeked of. He already hated being in places like that. He wanted to hurry up and leave while ensuring that Daleigh was going with him.

Daleigh sighed again as she plopped beside her mother's bed in the shared room. This was not what she had come to the hospital for. She just wanted to check on her mom and leave. The smell in the room added to the migraine she felt starting to brew in the back of her head and behind her eyelids.

"Yall, please don't start this mess again!" Daleigh was hitting her limit, and she had just stepped into the room.

"It's not me. It's them." Marcus retorted.

"No, it's him. I don't understand why you won't listen to me, Daleigh. This dude doesn't care anything about you. He wouldn't have caused your mom to break down again if he did." Jason was on the verge of yelling. He had had enough of Marcus butting in where he didn't belong. He was always trying to start something. Jason was the only one who could run the messy show. Marcus was not allowed to start any mess. He almost hated Marcus. He had come into Jason's daughter's life and shredded it. Jason was the only one who could control Daleigh. He knew Marcus was playing her like a violin. But would he prove it to her? How could he show her he and her mother were the only people she could trust to run her life? Oh, Jason didn't love his daughter. He liked her a lot. His heart just didn't allow him to love her. He loved Casey with his everything. She needed him like he needed her. She was so frail mentally. Daleigh was too strong and wouldn't let him and Casey's wildness dictate her life. They were not the center of her world.

Jason resented Daleigh for that. He was going to break her one way or another, he thought. The only person standing in the way of that was Marcus. Game recognized the game, and Jason recognized Marcus when Daleigh brought him home to meet them. Jason used to be one of those men. When he met Casey, he searched for a woman who would allow him to control her entire life. Casey had always been on the edge of insanity her whole life. She was neglected as a child. She always wanted people's attention and would do anything to get it. Jason was the same, but he controlled how people looked at him. He was never the center of attention at home. Where Casey was an only child, Jason had three brothers and two sisters. He was the youngest, so he had a lot of attention but wanted all of it. He was to be the center of attention in everyone's life. Daleigh was no exception. But how do you expose Marcus? Jason watched Marcus' face as he aimed to start the next level of pushing Casey over the edge.

"I don't know why you always accuse me of starting stuff. All I want to do is protect Daleigh. I love her. You're not good parents, and you know it. I can take better care of her than you ever did!!" Marcus had turned on a new gear and was going in for the kill shot. It may get them tossed out of the hospital, but he knew it would make Daleigh that much closer to him and dependent on him.

"GET OUT!!!" Casey screamed.

"Mom!!!" Daleigh screamed back. She could see things were getting out of hand, but she didn't know what to do about it. She wanted to please everyone, but that was not going to happen. She started trying to get Marcus to leave. "Come on, baby. Let's go. I don't want you all arguing again. It's been enough for today. It already put my mom here. She doesn't need another tranq."

"No!! I'm not going anywhere until this problem is fixed. I'm tired of your parents walking all over you and telling you what to do. You're an adult, and you should be treated like one. I don't appreciate them running your life." Marcus was geared up and going for the kill. "Daleigh, you need to decide now!! You either want me or your parents. You can't have both!!"

"Please don't do this, Marcus!!" Daleigh cried. She loved her parents despite how they treated her. She also loved Marcus and didn't want to leave him. She felt he was right about her parents controlling her life. At the same time, she was unsure about living with Marcus. Daleigh felt so confused and torn. She ran out of the room with tears streaming down her face.

Marcus smirked at Json and Casey. He knew he had won. He was the only one who could go after Daleigh and finish persuading her to his side. Jason and Casey would never get another chance to interfere with his control of Daleigh. Her father might have had the upper hand before but never battled anyone like Marcus. Marcus and Jason stared at each other in anger and hostility. Marcus smiled at Jason, turned on his heel, and marched out of the room. Jason knew things would go wrong, and he could do nothing.

The Big Chop

Daleigh ran out to Marcus' car, bawling. She couldn't believe Marcus and her father were arguing over her again. She was being forced to make a decision, and it was killing her inside. She loved her parents. She loved Marcus. Daleigh just wanted them to get along. Yet it was Marcus' fault that Casey was in the hospital as it was. He was constantly pushing buttons. He knew what it took to make people explode with just enough words and pushing the right buttons. Daleigh didn't understand why Marcus was this way.

Marcus strolled to the car. He knew Daleigh was probably already there waiting for him. He kept his face stoic, even though he was laughing inside. He had won this war. There were no more battles. Daleigh was putty in his hands. He was going to break her, mold her, destroy her. He had never dated a woman her age. She had a strong character, but her parents had broken her enough that it wasn't hard for Marcus to make her bend to his will. He arrived at Daleigh's side of the car and wrapped her in his arms.

"I'm so sorry, beautiful. I didn't know things were going to go that way. I didn't mean to make your mom and dad angry again."

"Why can't you all just get along?" cried Daleigh. Her head hurt so bad she felt she was going to pass out from the pain. Daleigh hadn't had a migraine in so long. She didn't even have her medicine with her. She didn't want to go back into the hospital, though. "Can we go home, please? My head is starting to hurt really bad."

"Yeah. Let's go home so you can take your meds." Marcus walked around to the driver's side and cranked up the car. He looked over at Daleigh. Daleigh didn't notice Marcus staring as she closed her eyes and leaned back. He had no intention of letting her take her migraine meds. She needed to suffer that pain for not listening to him. If Daleigh had just been obedient, her head wouldn't hurt. Marcus was so angry that she argued with him before her parents. She was going to pay a price.

Daleigh could feel the car start moving. She tried to let the window down so she could get some air, but her body was beginning to feel hot from the pain of the migraine. She realized the window wouldn't go down. Daleigh cracked her eyes to look over at Marcus. His face was steel. He was staring straight ahead like she wasn't in the car. Daleigh wanted to say something, but her mouth was dry and felt papery.

"I feel you looking at me. I don't know why. I have told you repeatedly, don't argue with me in front of people. You're supposed to have my back no matter what. Now you have a migraine. You're so stupid. Just when I think you're going to act right, you think. Stop thinking. It's not your strong suit. Let me handle things, and you just follow me. Got it?!!" Marcus' voice was calm but still cut like a knife.

"I'm sorry, Marcus," Daleigh whispered. "I didn't mean it. I was angry and didn't want my mom and dad to get hurt. I won't do it again. I promise."

"It's too late!!! You have disrespected me for the last time!!"

Daleigh didn't even see Marcus' hand coming. She just felt pain, then darkness.

Marcus looked over at Daleigh. They had pulled up to the house. He hadn't meant to hit her that hard. It was supposed to be just enough to remind her who was in control. Fortunately, there was no redness or swelling from the hit. He was going to have to be more careful next time. Daleigh had never been hit before by him. Marcus started to think of the proper excuse so Daleigh wouldn't realize what had happened. While he was thinking, Daleigh woke up.

"Hey, baby. Are you ok? You were saying something about your head, and then you passed out." Marcus hurriedly explained.

"I did? I don't remember," Daleigh murmured. Her head was still pounding. She felt like she had been hit by something; she just didn't know what because of the pain coming from the migraine. It felt strange, though, that the pain radiating from the migraine was not the same place another pain was coming from another part of her head. Daleigh was confused about what was going on.

"Here, I'll carry you in the house. You don't look so good." Marcus rushed to the passenger side of the car and picked up Daleigh. She grabbed her head. Even though the sun started falling, she still felt too bright outside. Marcus rushed to get her in the house. He knew eventually, she may figure out he had punched her. Daliegh was squirming in pain as Marcus placed her on the bed.

"Please be gentle, Marcus," Daleigh pleaded. "My head hurts really bad. Please get me my meds."

Marcus looked at her. If she thought he was still going to allow her to escape the pain of disrespecting him at the hospital, she was not going to get that relief. He stared at her face twisted in pain, reveling in the feeling of control of her agony. Marcus would let her suffer for another hour or two, then give her her meds. He couldn't describe the feeling it gave him to watch her writhe in pain. Daleigh eyes were tightly closed. Her body twisted from the pain. She couldn't even cry because that would cause more pain.

"Marcus. Please." Daliegh said quietly. She knew he could hear her. She could still smell that he was in the room. Daleigh just didn't know exactly where. She could also feel him watching her.

"I think you need to wait a little longer. I've warned you about disrespecting me, but you never seem to learn. But I got you today. Oh, and there will be no one to help you. I called your job and told them you quit. Your parents are blocked on your phone, so I changed the number. I think you'll behave from now on, won't you?" Marcus' voice sounded so sweet, yet the words dripped with venom and daggers. He wanted to cut her mentally and emotionally. She would never leave. She wouldn't want to.

Daleigh's mind was trying to process what was happening. Why had Marcus suddenly changed? He said he loved her and had no reason to treat her like this. She would think about it later because it hurt too much now. Time eventually crept by. Daleigh didn't know the time, but Marcus gave her her sumatriptan. He gave her the second dose not long after that. As Daleigh's pain decreased, she began to think about what was happening. How could she leave? She had nowhere to go. Marcus had intentionally destroyed her job. Her parents probably didn't want anything to do with her. What was going on?

Marcus was lying on the bed next to Daleigh as her head improved. He needed to tighten the ropes. He knew she could be strong-willed. She was also obedient. He saw the control Jason had over Casey. If he could make Daleigh like that, he may not have to find a new victim. This could be a long-term relationship. Marcus was sure Daleigh was in love with him. He didn't love her. He wasn't capable of it. His mother had ruined the chance of him ever loving a woman. He knew how to use them, though, just like his mother used him and every other man. Marcus had made sure she suffered for everything she had done to him and allowed it to be done to him. Every woman reminded him of his mother. Daleigh didn't, though. Maybe it was because of her age and innocence. No matter. Marcus had enough money saved to spend more time in Videl and keep an eye on Daleigh. He needed to make sure he was around her daily. It was the only way to keep her dependent on him and away from everyone else. Marcus' mind started to develop the perfect plan.

Daleigh woke up the next day feeling much better. Marcus had already gotten up, and she could smell the cooked food from the kitchen. She got up and headed to the shower. Somehow, Marcus had clothes in the closet for her, the right size and all. Daleigh wasn't sure how to feel about that. It seemed like Marcus was even controlling her style. Granted, she didn't have much, but she still wanted a choice in her clothes. Daleigh dressed and grabbed her phone on the way downstairs to the kitchen. She glanced at her phone to notice it was quiet. Her dad didn't call to update her on her mom. It seemed strange, but she didn't think much of it. Daleigh arrived at the table and smiled at Marcus.

"Good morning, babe. You feeling better?" Marcus asked as if nothing had happened.

Daleigh smiled at him. "I'm feeling 100% better. Thank you for taking care of me last night. I appreciate you."

Marcus stared at Daleigh, smiling. His mind was clicking, though. She still hadn't realized that he had punched her in the head. He was hoping no damage was done to Daleigh's head. The last thing Marcus needed was to try to explain anything to the police.

THE NEXT FEW WEEKS went by quietly. Daleigh's parents didn't attempt to get in touch with her. She figured they had decided to let things cool down. She did notice that Marcus barely left the house. If he left, he made sure Daleigh was going with him. Marcus told Daleigh she didn't have to worry about work anymore. He had taken care of everything. He felt she shouldn't have to work anymore since her migraines were so bad, and it wasn't safe to be out of his eyesight. Daleigh didn't even realize that Marcus was cutting her off from the world more and more. Her friends stopped contacting her. No one came by the house to check on her anymore. Daleigh was living in Marcus' created world.

Almost a year went by. Daleigh had her 19th birthday alone. Marcus paid her no attention that day. He didn't even buy her a present or cake. Daleigh was feeling more and more caged in. Marcus hadn't physically hit her again, but his words may as well have been punches. He destroyed her soul on purpose. He always told her how no one else would want her. Marcus took every chance to feed her lies, ignore her, and then love on her like he never did anything wrong to her. Daleigh was confused, and with no one to talk to, she was alone with her thoughts and confusion. She knew she needed to get away from Marcus somehow. There were no connections. Daleigh began to plan around the next time they went to the grocery store. Marcus never went to the one in town. He always went to the next city, so no one could see Daleigh or talk to her. Marcus also ensured the cities were large so they never visited the same store twice. He was in control and would do everything he could to keep it that way.

DALEIGH SAT IN THE car quietly. If she didn't run today, she may never get the chance again. Marcus had turned the music up in the car. It was a sound Daleigh hated and made her head hurt. She shut out the noise through meditation. She also found a way to contact others secretly through YouTube. Daleigh couldn't use social media because Marcus monitored everything. He knew what she did on her phone and who she spoke to. Yet he didn't monitor the videos she watched because he figured she couldn't do anything with those. Marcus didn't realize Daleigh was sending messages in the video comment sections. She had someone in the group monitor her location through the phone. It could only be done when away from the house because Marcus had the location blocked at the home, which would be dangerous. Daleigh was patient. She knew she had someone protecting her. She just had to trust them.

Marcus kept looking over at Daleigh. Her face wasn't twisted in pain from the music. If anything, it seemed like she had disconnected herself. He had noticed that over the past year, Daleigh had been disconnected mentally and emotionally from him. Marcus couldn't figure out how she did it, though. He made sure she was disconnected from everyone. He intentionally kept Daleigh alone. She was getting something from somewhere.

"Hand me your phone!!" Marcus demanded. Daleigh handed over the phone without saying anything. Marcus slowed the car down so he could look at it. He saw nothing suspicious, yet his cruel mind knew something was happening.

"You better not even try me. I promise you will regret it. I will break every bone in your body and leave you in the woods. Play with me if you want to." Marcus' voice was low. Yet it instilled a level of fear in Daleigh. Her mind started going over the plan again as Marcus threw the phone back at her without looking in her direction. All Daleigh had to do was let the person know what store they would be in. The group had already prepared the car, ID, clothes, and money for Daleigh. They just had to get her out.

Marcus and Daleigh pulled up to Walmart. Daleigh made a point not to glance around too much, which would arouse Marcus' suspicion. They walk around the store with a cart, picking up some items. Daleigh glanced down the water aisle, seeing her contact wave at her. She hurried and looked at Marcus to see he wasn't paying attention.

"I'm going to grab some water," Daleigh said, hoping Marcus would continue not paying attention.

"Yeah. Okay. Hurry up!!" Marcus said absently.

"I will. This will be the last time I ever see you." Daleigh thought. She walked down the aisle to her contact. Someone else approached Marcus and started a conversation. Daleigh connected with the contact, who moved her to the other end of the aisle to another person from the camera's view. She handed Daleigh a wig. Daleigh placed it on her head and ran towards the door—a black Toyota parked near the entrance with the keys in the ignition. She jumped in the car and sped off. She had dropped her phone in the trashcan on the way out the door so Marcus couldn't track her. Daleigh drove off quickly without looking back. The connection called the new phone in the car and told Daleigh that Marcus was searching for her in the store. She had already gotten far enough away that Marcus couldn't follow her. Daleigh said thank you and hung up the phone. She drove toward the sun. Another connection had sent her coordinates to the next destination, where she would change clothes and her hair.

Daleigh pulled into the hair salon. A prepaid money card was hidden in the car's middle console. She grabbed it and walked into the salon. Daleigh was about 100 miles from Videl. The salon also had a change of clothes hidden in the back for her to change into. There was a suitcase with clothes and more money. The salon connection would pass the next set of coordinates. Daleigh walked in, dreading cutting her hair. She knew that she needed the change, though. She walked into the salon. The connection recognized her immediately. She gestured for Daleigh to get into her chair. An hour later, Daleigh looked utterly different. Her hair was a gorgeous shade of red. It had been cut into short curls that shaped her round face. Her purple eyes popped. The connection did a soft makeup on Daleigh's face so as not to do too much. She looked and felt beautiful. Daleigh knew this was the beginning of a new start for her. She changed clothes, jumped into the grey Grand Prix, and rode off headed to the following coordinates.

New Growth

Daleigh pulled into the hotel to rest. She had traveled for almost 8 hours. The salon coordinate set up the hotel, and the hotel coordinate had the final set of coordinates for where Daleigh was supposed to stay permanently. There are still another 500 miles to that destination. Daleigh checked in with her luggage and walked to the room. She went to McDonald's and purchased some food. She didn't eat much because her nerves were still on edge. Even though she knew Marcus would have difficulty getting a trail on her, Daleigh was still afraid for her life.

Eventually, Daleigh fell asleep. There wasn't much rest. She began having nightmares about Marcus walking through the door and beating her. At some point, Daleigh gave up sleeping and checked out of the hotel. She went to the Starbucks down the street, then got back on the highway. Daleigh placed the final coordinates into the GPS. She traveled another 250 miles, then turned onto some back roads. These roads were going to lead to the final destination. The last stretch went without incident. Daleigh did check-ins hourly with the primary contact. The way this network worked was there was a primary contact. The primary arranged for connections in different places for the victim. The network had car dealerships, doctor's offices, social workers, salons, and more connections. There was a set final coordinate, usually in a small town, for the victim. The network ensured the final coordinates had a connection to assist the victims and keep an eye on them.

Daleigh pulled into the small rented home in Asdele. The city had only about 500 people and was small, quaint, and hidden. A road through the trees led into the town. Daleigh's new home was down a dirt road from the main road. The house was quaint. The exterior was painted blue and white. There were small bushes around the outside. The steps were brick. There was a small porch jutting from the front. The house looked homely and fit in well with the surrounding trees. The home was brick and wood. Daleigh got out of the car, stretching her tight muscles. The air smelled pure and like oak and pine. She couldn't believe that this place was going to be her home. A lady walked out of the house and toward Daleigh.

"Hi!! It's Janice. I'm your final connection, " the woman said as she reached out to Daleigh. Daleigh felt so at peace that she reached out to hug her, her body shaking with unreleased tears. Janice reached out and hugged Daleigh, feeling the release of the tension in her body.

"This poor girl," Janice thought. "She has been through so much. Baby girl, I promise to help you get through this."

Daleigh clung tightly to Janice, grateful for her hug and holding her. It felt like a huge weight was lifting off her shoulders. She had lived in so much fear during the ride. To see someone's face who cared did everything Daleigh's heart needed. Janice guided Daleigh into the house to sit down. The inside of the house was as quaint as the outside. There were two dark blue couches against the two walls. It was also a lazy chair by the front door. A man was sitting on the sofa, watching the door. He stood up quickly when Janice and Daleigh walked through the door. He saw Daleigh's tears and ran to get a tissue. He came back and shoved the tissue into Daleigh's hands. She grabbed them and started wiping her face. Janice guided Daleigh to the more oversized sofa.

"Sit down and calm down, sweetheart. It's ok. You're ok. He can't hurt you again." Janice consoled. She sat next to Daleigh. She pointed at the man. "This is my husband, James. He's here to help bring everything in and do any handy work."

"Hey!! Nice to meet you." James said as calmly as possible. He didn't want to cause Daleigh any more reactions.

"I'm so sorry. I didn't mean to scare y'all. I just had so much inside. I'm still scared that my ex will pull up any minute." Daleigh's voice shaking with fear.

"Baby girl, you don't have to worry about that. Just through the path is my and my husband's house. We are not too far. The alarms let us know if something goes wrong. There are cameras outside. His face is entered as a stranger and dangerous, so the computer will pick it up if he steps on the property. You're safe, sweetheart. I promise. We will do everything we can so you won't get hurt again." Janice lifted Daleigh's face with her finger so she could look into her eyes, encouraging her. "My!! Your eyes are so different. How did you get purple eyes?"

"I don't know. I don't think anyone on either side of my family has eyes like mine." Daleigh stated.

"Hmmm. Something about that doesn't feel right." Janice's mind began to wander. Daleigh's eye color was the same as someone Janice knew from the past. She couldn't remember who, though. Janice figured it would come to her later.

"Well, I'm going to lie down. I feel a migraine coming on. I have to find my meds." The pain could be heard in her voice and seen on her face. James hurried out to the car to get Daleigh's bags. He was concerned about her and Janice. He could see the look on his wife's face. He understood the concern she had about Daleigh. It matched his own. James could see this young woman needed love. He and Janice would do everything they could to help her heal. They were in for a long road ahead.

When James returned with the bags, Daleigh said, "Thank you for bringing my stuff." He placed them in the room on the right side down the hallway. It was the main bedroom. There was a bathroom down the hall on the left, right after the bathroom. The kitchen was toward the back of the house.

Daleigh hurried behind James so she could take her pills and lie down. Her head started pounding, and the lights became too bright for her eyes. Daleigh went into the darkened room, took her meds, and lay down. Janice and James walked to their home in the back. Janice strolled, it being obvious there was something on her mind.

"What are you thinking about baby?" James asked.

"Daleigh looks like someone I know. I'm just trying to remember who. And the pain that the baby is in. My heart hurts so much for her. To think that was me five years ago. The fear Daleigh is living in. I hope she sees Dr. Shelby soon. There is so much Baby Girl needs to heal from." Janice hugged herself as she reached the steps to their house. James opened the door and let Janice walk through first. He followed closely behind her, wrapping his arms around her and pulling her to him.

"Fortunately, she has us to help her through this. The community will help and protect her. I wish I could get my hands on this dude. I would whip his behind. I hope he never finds Daleigh. If he does, he will break her in every way possible." James said quietly.

"I KNOW WHO SHE LOOKS LIKE!!" Janice yelled suddenly. "She looks like Michelle. The girl that my ex Maison hurt and almost killed. Michelle had a little girl. But she disappeared. We thought Maison was the baby's father, but we never found out because he disappeared and he kidnapped the baby. Daleigh is about the right age. Her eye color is the same as Michelle's. I think Daleigh is her daughter.
"

"What happened to Michelle?" James asked.

"She passed somehow a couple of years ago. We don't know if Maison caught up to her or what. She was found dead not far outside of Chiva." Janice answered, a shiver running up her spine. No one from Chiva could understand what happened to Michelle. She was a beautiful girl. She was a single mother at 21 years old. Maison was believed to have been her boyfriend and the father of her child at some point, considering the baby looked just like him. Maison was abusive toward every woman who entered his field of vision, especially verbally. It could get physical quickly if you were in a relationship with him. There were several women he had placed in the hospital. The law couldn't control him, and he ensured all of Chiva knew about it. Maidon had broken Janice's jaw several times while dating her. When he disappeared with Michelle's daughter, everyone figured neither would ever show up again. Yet here was Daleigh.

Getting Started

Daleigh woke up the next morning feeling much better. She washed off since she didn't before lying down the day before. She then went to the kitchen to see what was in the fridge. Janice and James decided to fill up the refrigerator and freezer with everything Daleigh liked. She was very appreciative of their care and concern for her. She felt protected and loved by them. Jason and Casey never made Daleigh feel loved and treasured. She always felt like a pawn between themselves and the world. Marcus only valued her when it was to control her. Daleigh was finally free. And she planned to stay that way. She fixed some eggs, sausage, and homemade frozen biscuits. It seemed Janice had an affinity for baking. Daleigh took her breakfast to the table and ate quietly while doing some searching on her new phone. She was just finishing her food when she heard a knock on the back door.

"Hi! It's me!" Janice called through the screen. Daleigh hurried to the door and opened it for her. They hugged and then sat at the table.

"What's going on?" Daleigh asked.

"So, how much do you know about yourself?" Janice was straight to the point. She believed some questions needed to be answered sooner rather than later. Janice was now concerned for Daleigh twice. She feared Marcus was still a problem and that if Maison found out about Daleigh, there would be an even more significant issue. Janice needed to ensure everyone's safety. Having gone through the system of coordinators herself for her freedom, Janice knew that covering trails and burning all loose ends and bridges were necessary. It allowed each victim to move on safely. Janice wanted to protect Daleigh from any and everything. She felt like a mother to her even though she had just met her the day before. She and James never had the opportunity to have children because Maison had taken that from her. He had punched Janice in the abdomen several times. The mental and emotional damage was worse than the internal damage.

"I don't know anything. My parents have always been Jason and Casey Miller. No one has ever mentioned anything else. I know I felt like they hated me growing up. I was more of a verbal punching back to them. My dad, Jason, is controlling. My mom, Casey, is a mental breakdown walking. They are compatible. I don't think they ever loved me. I don't even remember any real baby pictures of me. " Daleigh sighed. She was tired just thinking about the situation. Yet she knew there was something not right with the situation.

"I'm going to do some digging," Janice stated, determined to find the answers. "What's your birthday?"

"August 25, 2002," Daleigh answered.

"Oh my God!!!" Janice thought. That was the same day Michelle's 3-month-old daughter and Maison disappeared. It couldn't just be a coincidence. There was more. Janice was ready to start following the trail.

Daleigh looked over at Janice thoughtfully. She didn't know what was on her mind, but she could see how her eyebrows were close together in deep thought. She was starting to get concerned, mainly because of the questions. Suddenly, something popped into Daleigh's head.

"There's a yellow Winnie the Pooh blanket that my parents say I loved as a baby. They said I loved being wrapped in it and would take it everywhere."

"Daleigh!! I think you may be the daughter of this girl I used to know!!" Janice yelled. The commotion was so loud that James ran into the house through the back door.

"What's happening?? What's wrong??!! Why are you screaming??!!" James started sputtering.

Daleigh looked from James to Janice like they had both grown two heads. There was no way her parents weren't her parents, right? It's not possible that they got her some other way. Daleigh felt confused and lost. She had run from one problem to run into an even bigger one. Janice's questions weren't making sense.

"I know this doesn't make sense to you," Janice stated as if she had heard what Daleigh was thinking. "I hope to have some answers by the end of the month. What do you plan on doing for work with that out the way? We have a few stores here and some empty shops."

"I want to go to school. Are there any six-month to one-year-long classes here? It's something I can do quickly and have fun with. I like decorating a lot," Daleigh said.

"There's a class for planning weddings and parties. It's only a few months long. Do you want to go to the rec center and sign up? They are in person but free for those who came in through the cooperation." Janice asked, excited that Daleigh would do something fun and unique. Daleigh is planning events to allow Janice's newly started baking business to explode. She wanted to develop a cooperation where other rescued women who came to the town could have a job and a chance to better themselves whether they stayed there or left.

"So, can you or Mr. James take me to the rec center?" Daleigh asked.

"First...call me Mr. James again. I'm just James. I may be older than you, but I ain't that old." James said with a specific tone that sounded fatherly in his voice.

"Yes, sir!!" Daleigh answered, smiling. It had been so long since she had smiled like that. She could tell that Janice and James wanted to help her.

"When are you going to see Dr. Shelby? You should start treatment as soon as possible. This parent thing may be something you need to discuss with her also," Janice encouraged.

"I'm going to call her later. I will be ready to start treatment in a day or two. I have so much I need to sort through mentally and emotionally." Daleigh stated. She was ready to start healing from the past and start a new future. The first thing she needed to do was get Marcus out of her system. It was the only way she would be able to move on. Marcus had too much control over her. Daleigh didn't know how long it would take but was willing to put it in.

Daleigh and Janice arrived at the rec center an hour later, ready to get down to business. Janice took her to the front desk to fill out the class paperwork as the secretary contacted the point of contact for enrollment. Daleigh was excited to start an actual career. She had always loved decorating things and putting together the perfect color schemes. Marcus would never let her do more with it. Jason and Casey wouldn't allow her to use her gifts more than to line their pockets. They made her take the job at the Waffle House to push her to make more money. Jason was bent on controlling what Daleigh did and didn't want her making enough money to leave. Event planning could bring in a lot of money. Waffle House didn't pay enough to cover much. Casey would take the chance to run off any potential clients with random mental breakdowns. When Marcus came into Daleigh's life, he intentionally picked fights to keep people away from her. He isolated Daleigh so she couldn't grow. She realized that these people never cared about her. All that mattered was how they could benefit from her.

"Make sure you contact Dr. Shelby while you're here," Janice reminded Daleigh. Dr. Shelby, the town's only psychologist, had her office in the same building, which made it easier to see clients who had children and could not afford extra childcare.

"Could you please make an appointment for me with Dr. Shelby?" Daleigh asked the secretary. I need to see her as soon as possible."

"Let me look and see what she has available. I think she has an opening for today." The secretary started tapping the keys on the keyboard. "Here we go. After talking to the enrollment clerk, you can see her if you want to stick around for a bit. I'm putting the appointment in the computer for you now."

"Thank you," Daleigh answered.

"I'm glad you can get all of this done today. I will stay with you so you don't feel alone. Thank you for your help, Clarice." Janice said.

"You're so welcome, Janice. Take good care of our newest member. We will treat you like family, Daleigh. There is no more need to worry," Clarice answered.

Daleigh and Janice began walking down the hall to the enrollment office. Daleigh had completed the enrollment information. She was excited to be starting classes in a few weeks. Janice knew so many people that they were passing by in the hall. She began introducing Daleigh to everyone. By the time they reached the enrollment office, Daleigh was sure that she would never have to be in fear again. Several of the people they met were related to Janice. Daleigh met her sister-in-law Sheila and a few of Janice's brother's nieces and nephews. The biggest surprise was when they arrived at the enrollment office.

"Hi, Aunt Janice," A handsome man greeted. Daleigh couldn't believe her eyes. She was standing before her as a man who took her breath away. Marcus hadn't even made her feel like that. Her eyes stared straight into the man's in shock, suddenly feeling shy. "Hi there. I didn't even notice you came in with my aunt. I'm David."

"David, this is Daleigh. She's here to sign up for the event planning course. She just arrived here in town through the coordination." Janice spoke for Daleigh because she could tell she wasn't able to speak for herself.

"H-hi." Daleigh stuttered. She would stop breathing permanently if she kept looking at this fine chocolate man. He looked about 6 feet tall, with broad shoulders and a muscular build. He could set a room on fire with his gaze.

"Nice to meet you, Daleigh. Let's get you signed up. You're going to love this course. It has a lot of information, and it isn't long. I hope you plan to host some events for the town. They are always looking for an event planner or coordinator." David realized he was starting to babble. He couldn't help it, though. Daleigh's purple eyes had him mesmerized. They looked vaguely familiar, too; David didn't know where he had seen eyes so purple.

"Nice to meet you, too. Umm....I'm looking forward to taking these classes. Maybe I can open up my own company or something doing event planning." Daleigh blushed. Her face felt hotter than the Carolina Reaper pepper. She had never fallen in crush before. Daleigh was feeling scared of what she was feeling.

"So that does it. You're enrolled. You may want to check things on your birth certificate, though. Your age doesn't add up." David stated.

"What do you mean?" asked Janice.

"What I mean is that Daleigh's social popped in the system. She needs to see what's going on." Jason stated.

Daleigh began to become concerned. Why would her social media account pop up in the system? Was something really going on? As Daleigh wondered what was happening, Janice moved to her side.

"Are you ok, love?" Janice's voice was concerned.

"No. Let's go. I need to talk to Dr. Shelby. This isn't right!!" Daleigh said, rushing out of the office. Janice ran behind her and guided her to Dr. Shelby's office. Daleigh hurried through the door, not even checking in with the secretary.

"Wait for me!!" Janice said, waving at the secretary to check them in. She was worried about where things were about to go.

Twisted

"Dr. Shelby!! Dr. Shelby!!" Daleigh called. She opened the door to the office. Daleigh realized she was starting to panic. Her mind couldn't comprehend what was going on. Her breath was beginning to become shallow. She felt she was about to pass out. Janice saw Daleigh starting to stagger and ran to catch her. Dr. Shelby jumped out of her chair, running also to catch Daleigh. They sat her down, placing her head between her knees.

"Inhale....2, 3, 4, 5. Exhale...2, 3, 4, 5. Inhale 2, 3, 4, 5. Exhale 2, 3, 4, 5. Janice...What happened?" Dr Shelby instructed Daleigh and asked Janice questions at the same time.

"She just found out her social security number was flagged in the system from David. Something happened when he put her information in for enrollment." Janice explained.

"Daleigh, how are you feeling, honey?" Dr. Shelby asked. The secretary had told her who was coming in as Daleigh had run past her. She was very concerned about Daleigh's reaction and her hyperventilating. It seems too much happened at one time. Daleigh's mind was not ready for all of this. Dr. Shelby realized that the plan of action and tests she wanted to do first would not work. She needed to reassess Daleigh.

"Ok, Daleigh. Are you ready to get up and move to the office?" Daliegh's breath had finally evened out, and she didn't look like she would pass out anymore. Dr. Sheby and Janice helped her get up.

Daleigh moved to the office quickly. She sat in the chair and tried to give Dr. Shelby time to enter the office. As soon as she heard footsteps, she began spilling her soul.

"I'm so confused. I don't understand. My life with my parents was chaotic. Then I met Marcus. Then I found out today that there's something wrong with my life. What is happening to me? Why is this happening to me?!!" Daleigh felt her words were jumbled together.

"Slow down, slow down." coaxed Dr. Shelby. She hurried to her desk, turned on her recorder, and grabbed her notepad and pen. She had encouraged Janice to wait in the waiting room instead of entering the office. If Daleigh needed her, she could tell the secretary to send Janice back.

"I'm sorry. It seems like I'm always having to apologize." Daleigh stated. "I just need to get this off my chest before I explode. I'm fighting for my life here!!" Daleigh suddenly burst into tears.

Dr. Shelby considered how Daleigh's emotions were rapidly changing. That wasn't good. She could tell Daleigh had not been able to process everything emotionally. There was too much coming at her at one time. She walked over and gave Daleigh some tissue. Dr. Shelby hugged her back when she reached out for a hug. She then opened the door and called for Janice. Janice ran to the office. She quickly dropped to her knees to comfort Daleigh when she saw how hard she was crying.

"It's ok, baby girl. I promise it is. Let it out. It's ok." Janice consoled.

Daleigh started calming down again in Janice's arms. The release was what she needed. She thought she had let everything go the day before, but she had really let it go. Daleigh couldn't remember the last time she cried like that. The last time she felt safe enough to cry like that...well, it had never happened.

"My parents would never let me cry. If I cried, I would be sent to my room. I had to be perfect in front of them. I never got the chance to attach to them. I was never hugged. My grades had to be perfect. My clothes were never my choice. I couldn't speak but on certain things.

They controlled my life. Then Marcus came along. He was worse than them. I think at one point he hit me." Daleigh poured.

Dr. Shelby had been doing this job for a long time. She had never heard someone sound so torn. Daleigh's voice was just above a whisper. She didn't sound dead inside, but she sounded like she was dying. Dr. Shelby and Janice looked at one another. Daleigh's treatment was going to take a lot of time. Janice wanted to scream. She hated that this young woman was hurting so badly and there was nothing she could do about it.

Dr. Shelby closed her door. "This room is where it is so no noise can be heard in the hall. I want you to scream as loud as you can, Daleigh."

"AAAAAHHHHHH!!!!" Daleigh let go.

"AAAHHHH!!!" Janice screamed with her.

"There you go. Let it go. Now inhale 2, 3, 4.....exhale 2, 3, 4. Inhale 2, 3, 4....exhale 2,3, 4. Good job Daleigh." Dr. Shelby looked at the clock. Several hours had passed. "Let's end for today. Next week we'll pick back up and I'll let you know what tests we need to do so I can have a full assessment. Right now you're under a lot of stress. I don't want you to push yourself any further."

"Yes, Dr. Shelby." Daleigh readily agreed. She just wanted to go home and lie down. Just as Daleigh stood up, she suddenly got dizzy. The last thing she remembered was the panic on Janice and Dr. Shelby's faces before everything became black.

DALEIGH WOKE UP IN the hospital. Her head was pounding. She opened her eyes just enough to see the room. It was pristine. Daleigh then realized the beeping sound. She was in the hospital. She felt movement beside her. Janice lifted her head, James sitting next to her.

"What happened? Why am I in the hospital?" Daleigh asked.

David leaned close to her. She didn't realize he was in the room. It felt like the room was a little smaller with his 6-foot frame standing there.

"You passed out in Dr. Shelby's office. My aunt called me to carry you to the hospital." David informed Daleigh. At that moment, Dr. Shelby and another doctor walked in. Both of them had concern on their faces. It seems as if the atmosphere had changed and dropped several degrees. Daleigh looked at everyone around her. They all had the same expression of concern and fear she did.

"Daleigh, is it ok if we have everyone leave so we can talk to you?" Dr. Shelby asked, trying to keep her voice pleasant and not cause panic.

"Can Janice please stay?" Daleigh asked.

"If you're ok with that." The other doctor answered. David and James left the room. Daleigh grabbed Janice's hand.

"So Daleigh, when did the migraines start?" Dr. Shelby asked.

"I was really young. Probably around 6 or 7 years old. Why?" Daleigh was starting to get very nervous.

"There are several healed fractures towards the back of your skull. There is also a very recent crack to your jaw. It happened approximately 6 months ago." Dr. Shelby explained.

"Was I beaten or dropped or something?" Daleigh was worrying again.

"It looks like there has been some abuse. Do you remember anything?" Dr. Shelby was becoming concerned because Daleigh's blood pressure and heart rate were starting to go up.

"No!! I don't remember any of it. Why would anyone hurt me like that? Who would hurt me like that?!!" Daleigh was starting to become erratic again. The other doctor pulled out a syringe and gave Daleigh an injection to calm her down. Janice held her with tears streaming down her face. She understood Daleigh because she had been just as broken when she arrived in Asdele. Janice felt helpless when it came to Daleigh. She felt she may have pushed Daleigh by telling her about her possibly being kidnapped. Daleigh had calmed down because of the medicine. Janice was concerned though that Daleigh's mind may be more damaged from the situation.

"How is she?" David had come back into the room. He stared at Daleigh. His heart wanted to hug her close. He couldn't explain what he was feeling. Usually, he didn't want to get too close to people, but Daleigh made him want to get close to her. It wasn't that he wanted to heal her, but that she wanted to just be there for her in any way she needed him.

"She was so broken. I shouldn't have said anything until I had more evidence when it came to her family. Then, finding out that there was some type of damage to her head was the final straw. I don't know if she's going to come out of this, David. I'm scared for her." Janice's voice trembled with pain, fear, and tears. David had not seen his aunt in this condition in a long time. He was around five years old when Janice came home to them, broken. Janice was David's father Dennis's sister. His only sibling. Dennis was hurt when his sister returned home battered, abused, and with the loss of her ability to ever have children. If it hadn't been for James coming along, Janice might have been permanently loss in the pain and misery. She had gone through extensive therapy for a year before she could truly put her life back together. James with there with her every step of the way. David wanted to be to Daleigh what James was to Janice. But would she let him in?

DALEIGH WOKE UP TO David next to her bed instead of Janice. She looked at how his 6-foot frame didn't fit into the chair. She thought his body had to be cramping. As if David felt Daleigh, he slowly opened his eyes and then stretched. He had already been listening for Daleigh to wake up. He caught her staring at him.

"What's on your mind?" David asked with a smile on his face.

"No-nothing. Just admiring you." Daleigh stuttered, flustered at being caught. "Why are you sitting here instead of Janice?"

"She asked me to look after you. Uncle James took her home to rest. She is feeling bad about what happened and what she told you. Aunt Janice thinks she pushed you too far." David glanced at Daleigh in concern. He wanted to be sure the conversation didn't stimulate her again.

"I'm ok. I promise. No more freaking out. I'm better now. My mind just had a hard time processing everything. I want to do a paternity test with my parents. At the same time, I don't want them to know where I am. If they find out where I am, Marcus will find out. That's my biggest fear. I want to start my life here. I don't want him nor my parents anymore." Daleigh was very adamant.

"I can arrange for Dr. Shelby to help you with some of these. I will protect you as much as possible. You already know Aunt Janice will do anything for you. Uncle James is right there with her. Most of our family lives here, and they will protect you too. I have a few cousins on the police force. You're safe here. As safe as we can possibly keep you. I can't say that your ex won't try to find you. He probably will. But we will do everything we can to keep you hidden from him." David promised. Daleigh threw her arms around David's neck. Both of their hearts seemed to stop at that moment. It was as if time had stood still. His big arms around her felt safe. Daleigh couldn't understand why he felt so different from Marcus. She began to question if her feelings for Marcus were ever real, or just forced because of the situation with her parents and wanting to run away from them. Daleigh figured she could figure that out later with Dr. Shelby. She relished in the moment. At some point, she would thank David for this moment, but right now she just wanted to enjoy it.

Locced In

Marcus was livid!! He had spent days looking for Daleigh. Jason and Casey were no help. When he found out who helped her, he was going to make sure they never helped anyone else again. The question was: how did she get help? How did she find someone to contact? Something wasn't adding up for Marcus. He needed some help. Time to call his buddy Maison. If anyone could help he could. Daleigh was going to pay the price for disobeying him.

"Hey Maison. What's good buddy?" Marcus tried to hide the irritation in his voice.

"Why are you calling me? You got what you wanted. I put that girl on a silver platter for you. You done controlled every other girl. Why couldn't you control her?" Maison had a lot of animosity in his voice. He couldn't stand Marcus. That man was a failure in his eyes and a sorry piece of crap. Maison had given the man his daughter to keep, and he couldn't even control her.

"Man look. I had her on lock. Then she got away. I don't know where she went, man. I don't know how she got away." Marcus was starting to feel nervous. He didn't like the way Maison sounded.

"Where you at?" Maison demanded. Marcus gave him the address, and Maison jumped in his car. His violet eyes turned dark. He didn't care what needed to happen. Daleigh could not be found by anyone else. If anyone found out that he had kidnapped her and was the reason why her mother was dead, he was dead. He didn't even have to think about prison. All Marcus had to do was control her. Stupid idiot couldn't be trusted. Michelle had been a thorn in his side. She and Janice were the two women he had had the hardest time controlling. He knew he wouldn't have been able to control Daleigh the same way because she was his daughter. He didn't love her. He really didn't want her. Yet, she was the part of Michelle he could do something about. Michelle went crazy mentally when Daleigh was taken from her. Maison knew it was the thing to break her. He may have not gotten to see her broken, but he was glad it broke her. Janice on the other hand was another story. Maison had heard she was married and moved on with life. He had wanted to break her just as bad as he had Michelle. But Michelle was why he couldn't break Janice. She had helped her escape. If he could get his hands on Janice one more time, he would break her to the bone. Literally and figuratively.

While in his thoughts, Maison arrived at Marcus' house. They lived only a few hours from each other. Maison wanted to be close but not too close so he could keep up with Daliegh. Now to deal with Marcus. He knocked on the door.

"I'm coming!!" Marcus yelled. He opened the door to an extremely angry Maison. "Oh, man!! You got here fast. Ummm...come on in."

Maison punched Marcus in the face as soon as he walked through the door. "What's wrong with you bruh? You just up and let her leave? I told you to keep her close to you. You stupid bruh!!" Maison's face turned red with anger. Marcus knew he was in big trouble.

"Look, man. I didn't know the heifa was gone figure out a way to leave. She looked stupid. I know she ain't as bright as us. Plus, I kept her away from everyone else for the past 6 months. Ain't nobody come looking for her. She ain't have no social media. All I let her watch are videos."

Maison's rage was growing. "Stupid!!! Don't you know all she had to do was find some videos about being controlled or some people under the videos?!! You are the dumbest dude I know!!"

"Ay, man. I didn't see any comments under them videos. I checked." Marcus said.

"But I checked. She was talking to some people—a cooperation. I'm going to investigate how this thing works. I still have some police in my pocket from back home. You better make sure your stupid behind doesn't do anything while I figure this out." Maison turned to leave.

"A dawg. Let me help. I'm pretty sure I still got some connections too." Marcus was eager to help. He just wanted Daleigh back. She was like the perfectly wrapped present. Pretty eyes and face. Nothing like her father. His purple eyes were always cold and violent. Marcus could make a woman fear him, but not the way Maison did. Marcus was even scared of Maison. He would never tell him that though. He was too much of a man for that.

Marcus got down to business, looking at every video in the watch history on YouTube. He realized Daleigh watched a lot of videos. But was that on purpose? Did it hide the secret to how Daleigh got away? Marcus kept scrolling.

"Man, give me the computer. You taking too long. This chick needs to be found before somebody figures out what we doing." Maison gave his phone to Marcus so he could log into YouTube from his end. Maison started going through the videos also, looking more for the ones that dealt with abuse or domestic violence. He felt those were the ones that Daleigh would have used. That was how Janice and Michelle got away. They had used Myspace to do the same thing. As Maison was checking the comment sections, he noticed something under some of the videos. There was a girl named Purple Eyes who would make small comments. Her comments would be "Boyfriend acts like this" or "Needing help". There would be answers to her comments like "cooperation" and "underground escape". Maison figured the way to find Daleigh was to create a fake page. He needed to get in touch with his twin Chaison. Chaison knew more about social media and YouTube.

Maison and Chaison were 42 years old to Marcus almost 40 years of age. None of them looked their age though. They all knew they were handsome, and could get anything they wanted. Maison and Chaison had met Marcus in Chiva. The identical twins had run that town. Marcus had come through while driving trucks. This connection created a bad boys group that no one could control. If there was a woman they wanted, they would get her, destroy her, and leave her life in shambles. It was a surprise there were no women left in Chiva after the men's reign of terror came to an end. Marcus moved on to Videl with the promise of having access to Daleigh from Maison. Maison had taken Daleigh from Michelle to be given to Jason and Casey. Chaison had gone on to some unknown city, but Maison only had to type a short message, and the bat signal was sent.

Chaison showed up around 20 minutes later. Maison didn't know how he got there that fast and wasn't trying to find out.

"What's up, Bro??!!" Chaison smirked when Maison opened the door. Maison didn't want Marcus near Chaison because he needed business taken care of when it came to Daleigh. Marcus was too invested in the girl. Chaison cared nothing about his niece and honestly wished the girl didn't exist. He felt his brother did too much for her, and giving her to Marcus was the biggest mistake ever. But Maison was older, even though it was just by a few minutes.

"What's good man?" Maison answered, glad to see his brother. "Here's the computer. What can you do with it?"

Chaison's smile matched Maison's, a scary sight, one that scared even Marcus, as evil as he was.

"I think we need to ramp our game up brother!!" Chaison smiled. "We're going to create our own female profile and trace Daleigh's steps. Get rid of her when we find her. She's been a thorn in the side. Those stupid people you gave her to couldn't control her. Marcus couldn't control her. She has to be erased before they find out about Michelle."

No one knew how Michelle had died. Maison had hit her that day, leaving her in a ditch for dead. The body was found and was buried near the city. Even though people knew that Maison and Michelle were together, what they didn't know was that Chaison had chosen her for himself. He hated Michelle for being with Maison but hated Maison even more for taking Michelle knowing that she was the person he actually loved. Chaison had loved Michelle since they were in high school. He would be cruel to other girls, but if Michelle asked, he would leave them alone. Maison was never that type of person. He hated women and made sure they knew he did. Maison also didn't know a little secret. Daleigh wasn't his daughter. She was Chaison's daughter. For one moment Michelle belonged to Chaison after she ran to him from Maison hurting her. Maison knew her torture was Chaison's torture. Chaison agreed to have Daliegh removed for her safety. Maison would never know what they had done behind his back. The secrets Chaison held...

"I created the profile. We should be able to make contact with the cooperation. Give me a few days and I will find the trail." Chaison was typing away on the computer. Maison and Marcus rubbed their hands together. Now to wait.

CHAISON CHASED DOWN leads the next few days. He posted under several videos until he found what he was looking for. Some people connected him with the cooperation. Chaison had used a picture of a young woman through AI that couldn't be traced. Chaison had mastered computers at a young age. If it had a digital footprint, he could find it. He began hacking some of the systems. Chaison was having a hard time because a lot of what was done was not online. He thought this would be easy. Granted, he wanted to protect Daleigh. Yet, he needed to keep control of the situation. Maison and Marcus were smart, but not as smart as Chaison. He was going to send them around in circles until he could do something to keep Daleigh safe. He had to process both issues at once.

"I found a lead. Marcus, you go check it out. It's back in Chiva. It's one of the stops for the cooperation. Maison, go with him and see if you can find the people on this list since we know the town. It shouldn't be too hard." Chaison gave quick instructions. "I will keep on the path I'm on and keep y'all up to date through texts and calls."

"Alrigh," Marcus and Maison agreed. Maison had a feeling something was off though. He just couldn't put his finger on it. Chaison was up to something. Call it twin intuition, or just something abnormal. He wanted to stick close to his twin until he figured it out. Yet, he needed to find Daleigh even more. Marcus needed his pet back. Maison had destroyed Jason and Casey earlier that day. There was no way they would interfere in the search. Their names couldn't even be found anywhere. Casey was in a psych ward deep in the country. Jason...would never be found. Maison had his signature smirk on his face again. Things were finally getting back under his control. Marcus was easy to control because he always picked the weakest women. Chaison....Chaison was a different story. No matter what, Maison couldn't control him....except for Michelle. Maison smiled ruthlessly. Daleigh was a part of him and Michelle. If he could control her, his brother would come to heel. The only one that could be in charge was Maison...twin or no twin.

Everyone went their separate ways. Chaison didn't tell Marcus and Maison that he had found out about Daleigh and where she was. He jumped into his truck after ensuring that Maison and Marcus had gone in the other direction. He felt nervous for a while. He didn't know if Maison would trust him. But it's all he had. Chaison headed in the direction of Asdele. What he didn't realize was Maison was sitting at the end of the road, turning on the highway to follow his twin.

Growing It Out

Daleigh had finally been able to start going on with her life. Over the next few months, she had been in therapy with Dr. Shelby. David, Janice, and James had been trying to find information about her real parents. It was becoming a struggle because nothing was reported about a baby missing. They had dug into archives in surrounding counties. David's cousin who worked on the police force was also trying to find information on his end.

Daleigh enjoyed her decorating classes. She was planning to open a venue shop so she could create for clients. She found herself looking forward to the end of class because David would come by and pick her up for lunch and take her home before finishing his day at work. Daleigh was glad to have David around. Their relationship was growing. Janice and James were like her parents. Janice made a point to ensure that Daleigh had someone to talk to. James always gave her fatherly advice and guidance. Everyone in her life was taking care of her.

The sessions with Dr. Shelby were helping so much. Daleigh was able to get through the pain and turmoil in her life. Dr. Shelby also incorporated Janice in some of the therapies as a lifeline for Daleigh. She was journaling about the past and the thoughts of not knowing who her parent actually was. She wanted to reach out to Jason and Casey with questions but wasn't sure if that was safe or not, especially considering Marcus. She knew he could be extremely dangerous. She was glad she had left.

DAVID RECEIVED A CALL from his Jackson cousin at the police department. "What's up, man?"

Jackson answered, " Nothin much cuz. I got some information and I think you need to bring Daleigh in. Maybe Aunt Janice and Uncle James too."

"What's wrong?" David questioned, his chest feeling tight.

"Just bring everyone in. Even better, I'll meet you all at Auntie and Uncle's house. It may not be safe to tell you the news here at the office" Jackson muttered into the phone. He was concerned because he heard that Marcus was in Chiva looking for Daleigh's whereabouts. That meant Maison and Chaison weren't far behind. Those men were heinous criminals and as a group had caused so many problems in Chiva and surrounding cities. Marcus's driving trucks left destruction in many states. The police had been trying to track them down for years. Michelle's death was a reason why detectives were looking even harder for the crew.

Jackson arrived at his aunt and uncle's house. He felt a little nervous because of the situation. He had talked to his boss about the information he would share. Jackson wanted to make sure that all I's were dotted and all T's crossed. This case was about to take a turn no one expected. Jackson took a deep breath, then knocked on the door.

"Come in!!" Janice yelled.

"Hey everyone." Jackson greeted. David was sitting next to Daleigh on the sofa. James was sitting in his reclining chair. There was another reclining chair across from it that Jackson sat in. You would think Jackson and David were twins because of how their body shapes and faces looked. Yet Jackson was two years older than David at 24 to David's 22. All the men glanced at one another, knowing that a big moment was about to come. Daleigh couldn't be still, feeling anxious and like a rock was sitting on her chest.

"Ok, everyone. I have drinks, snacks, and tissues. Anyone need anything else?" Janice walked into the living room, realizing that the room felt a little staunch and cold. The air conditioner wasn't on as the weather was just right to leave the windows open. Yet it seemed as if things had become depressing. "So, I take it we're about to hear something we don't want to hear." Janice sat on the other side of Daleigh, grabbing her hand to help her calm down.

Jackson looked at everyone in the room, then placed his sight on Daleigh. "Daleigh, from what we know, you were definitely kidnapped as a baby. It's believed that you were kidnapped by a man named Maison Carter, who is also probably your father. He has an identical twin named Chaison. They ran with a guy named Marcus. Daleigh, Marcus is the one who hurt you."

Daleigh's eyes almost bulged out of her head. "Marcus is only 23. How could he be hanging out with guys that much older?"

"Marcus is almost 40. He's around the same age as Maison and Chaison." Jackson hated telling Daleigh this part because she had just gotten over the pain of what Marcus had subjected her to and the probable abuse of who she had believed were her parents.

David grabbed Daleigh as she slumped in tears. The anguish could be heard in her sobs. He couldn't believe someone who claimed to be a man could do something like that to a young woman. These men were sick. When Daleigh finally calmed down, Jackson continued.

"It looks like you were given to Jason and Casey to care for. From the examination of your X-rays and CT scan, a lot of the damage to your head was done as a baby. There's also a very recent injury, a small crack in your jaw. Did Marcus ever hit you?" Jackson questioned.

Daleigh shook her head. "No. Not that I know of. I do know there was one day when I had a migraine when coming back from seeing my mom....I mean Casey in the hospital. Marcus wasn't happy with how I spoke to him. I had closed my eyes because of the pain while we were driving. I thought I passed out from that because that's what Marcus told me. Are you telling me he actually hit me? He may have punched me?"

"It doesn't take much force to cause the injury you have." Jackson shook his head. "We've also been told that he's back in Chiva asking questions. He's looking for you. If he's looking, Maison probably isn't too far behind. We would rather you stay in a safe house or with Aunt Janice until we can catch these guys. Your life is in danger again."

He watched with sympathetic eyes as Daleigh began to shake like a leaf. David was holding her hand, wincing as her grip kept tightening as Jackson talked. David wished he could erase all of her pain. All he could was love her through it and support her. He knew he couldn't get rid of these men single-handedly. David had to allow his cousin and the other police officers to do their job.

Janice and James looked at each other. The blessing was that they had extra rooms in their house. They also had a basement, and the car garage was attached to the house and could only open and close by a special remote. James had all of this done when he and Janice married so she could be protected if Maison ever came looking for her. Now, Maison was on a warpath, and so was Marcus. Chaison was probably part of the problem, but may not be a player in the game. Either way, David was going to do everything he could to protect Daleigh. He had fallen in love with her, but he knew all of the wounds in her heart needed to heal before he could make a move to start dating her. David knew the people of Asdele would do everything possible to help Daleigh.

"I'm going to make a call." David stepped out of the front door. He reached into his pocket for his phone and dialed Dr. Shelby. "Hey, Doc. I was wondering if you could come to my Aunt Janice's house. Daleigh just got some heavy news, and I know she's been working to deal with things. I think your presence would be helpful and guide her through this mess. She's not doing too good."

"I'll be there in about 15 minutes." Dr. Shelby said. She was concerned about Daleigh's reaction. She knew part of what Jackson was explaining as she helped with reading the medical images. Jackson had consulted her before going to Daleigh with the information he and other detectives had found. Dr. Shelby knew Daleigh was as prepared as possible mentally for what was about to happen. The physical had healed, but the mental and emotional still had a long way to go in healing and coping. Having Janice, James, and David by her side was the biggest support. Dr. Shelby wanted to do more, but it wasn't time for her to play her hand yet.

Dr. Shelby pulled up to the house in 10 minutes. She ran inside, not even bothering to knock on the door. Daleigh heard her and ran to her. Dr. Shelby wrapped her in her arms and just swayed side to side. The entire room as quiet as Dr. Shelby soothed Daleigh's cries. When she was finally calm enough, she led her back to the sofa. Janice moved to sit with James so Dr. Shelby could sit next to Daleigh with David on the other side. They both grabbed one of her hands and then looked at Jackson to continue.

"So, Dr. Shelby ordered a DNA test. Umm...the results were what we expected but not what we expected. You are Michelle's daughter. You're also the daughter of Chaison and Maison Carter." Jackson looked down at the DNA result paper in his hand, feeling the eyes of every shift to him. What was happening? "Chaison and Maison are identical twins. Therefore their DNA is almost exactly the same. We have sent everything off to another lab to do deeper testing."

Janice's eyes were huge. She turned to look at James who's eyes were almost as big as hers. David pulled Daleigh closer as Dr. Shelby's grip on Daleigh's hand was so tight her fingers were darkening around the knuckles. No one glanced at Daleigh's face for fear of what they would see. The color had left her face. It was as if someone had sucked all the air out of the room. David heard the change in her breath and pulled her close. Dr. Shelby's breath also changed. She felt as faint as Daleigh did. The shock in the room was palpable.

"Is it ok if I continue?" Jackson asked after clearing his throat, clearly feeling uncomfortable.

"P-p-please," Daliegh answered, her head buried in David's chest. Everyone else just nodded in agreement.

"Alrighty then. So, it seems there's another mystery added to this. Michelle was believed to be dead. Now there's evidence that says she might not be." Jackson continued. Both Dr. Shelby and Janice took a sharp breath. They looked at one another, then looked away. Anyone paying attention would have noticed how both women's bodies stiffened. Bother knew a lot more than they would ever tell.

"Well, we're going to continue this investigation. We have a lead on Marcus. We have not been able to track down Chaison or Maison. I'm concerned because if any of them can find you, Daleigh, it might be something we can't control. We have stepped out patrols out here. Why don't you maybe move in with my Aunt Maxine and Uncle Dennis, David's parents? I would feel better if you were in town instead of out here in the country. The same goes for you, Aunt Janice and Uncle James. It easier to keep Daleigh safe if we are all near each other." Jackson urged.

All the women nodded their heads. Everyone in the room realized the gravity of the situation. There was a set of twins and a madman who wanted Daleigh back. Safety meant numbers and moving quietly.

"David, why don't you walk with Daleigh to her house so she can pack some clothes and get other things she needs." Janice was the first to speak. She really thought she had escaped Maison, but this man seemed to be bent on ruining lives, even if it meant destroying his own flesh and blood. It scared Janice. Knowing how long it had taken for her to recover and Daleigh's own recovery journey, they each had to make the best choices.

"Sure Auntie," David answered. "Come on Daleigh. Let's make this quick. I want to get you to my parent's house as soon as possible." Daleigh nodded her head, then got up slowly. Dr. Shelby still seemed a bit shell-shocked. She needed to make sure she was distant from Daleigh, yet close enough to protect her if needed. If Maison and Chaison wanted to return, then she would have something waiting for them. Marcus had gained himself a spot on the "mess around and find out" list. Based on what Daleigh had told her through therapy, Marcus was almost identical to Maison in how they treated women. She wanted to keep Asdele from ending up like Chiva.

Jackson's phone rang, so he stepped out to take the call. David and Daleigh followed behind headed toward the house Daleigh was in. David placed his arm around Daleigh's shoulder. She flinched without thinking about it. David noticed, and so he removed his arm and just touched her hand.

"I'm sorry. You can place your arm around me. Hearing the news just made me feel a little sensitive." Daleigh explained. She leaned her head on David's shoulder. David placed his arm around Daleigh as they entered her house.

"I'm going to pack really quick. I'll be right back," Daleigh informed David. He stood outside her room door, being able to see the front and back doors from that spot. He was concerned these men were too close. Granted Janice and Dr. Shelby had gone through great lengths to hide Daleigh and her identity. The cooperation did the same. David just felt there was something off, he just didn't know how to put his finger on it. His head lifted toward Daleigh as she pulled her suitcase out of the room.

"I gotchu. I'm so sorry that you're having to go through this. I know your life is unhinged again. But let my family protect you. We won't let anything happen. We will take care of you, I promise." David said.

"I know you and your family will. Janice and James have never gone back on their word. You may be new in my life, but you have never made me feel unsafe. I actually like you. I'm looking forward to maybe spending more time with you when this is all over. I just need this to get all of this over with so my life can be put back together." Daleigh mumbled to David.

"There is no rush. I just want you to have peace. I'm here for you, for anything you need. You've almost finished your classes. You're moving forward. I'm sorry that Marcus hurt you like he did. I'm also sorry that you don't have the answers you need. I will hold your hand through it all though." David grabbed Daleigh's suitcase and headed to his truck. They got in, and Janice, James, and Dr. Shelby followed them to Dennis and Maxine's house. Jackson had already left in his car.

EVERYONE GOT OUT OF their vehicles. Maxine and Dennis came out to meet them. David had already sent them a message saying what was going on. Dennis did not want Maison near his sister again. He knew James would protect her the way he would and then some. Then he turned his concern to Daleigh. Dennis and Maxine knew David cared a lot about Daleigh. She was all he ever talked about. It hurt his heart to know how the people who were supposed to be her parents treated her. It made him even angrier that Marcus had treated Daleigh like Maison had treated Janice. But he was going to do everything he could to help David, Janice, James, and Dr. Shelby keep Daleigh safe.

"Everyone come on in." Maxine encouraged. Everyone follows her into the house. "Daleigh, do you want something to snack on or do you want to wait until later?"

"I'll wait until later. My head is starting to hurt really bad." Daleigh was struggling against passing out. She hadn't had a bad migraine in a long time. She figured the stress of the day had brought it on. She just needed to medicate and lie down for a little while. Janice handed Daleigh a bottle of water. Maxine guided Daleigh to the room she would be staying in temporarily, David not far behind with her luggage.

"Here sweetheart. Lie down for a while. I'll close the door so you can have some privacy." Maxine said.

"I'll be right downstairs. All you have to do is call me and I'll come." David said, his voice feeling distant. Daleigh knew he had a lot to chew on from the conversation with Jackson.

"Thank you, Mrs. Dobson. Thank you, David." Daleigh lay in the bed, pulling the blanket over her head. David and Maxine closed the door.

"What's on your mind, David Michael Dobson? I know you. And I know you want to hurt that man. He isn't worth it, son. You have a lot going for you. You're helping Daleigh get better. The best thing you can do is be here for her and protect her," Maxine consoled.

"I know, Mom. It's just hard to sit in the background. I would rather be out with Jackson trying to find these dudes. It's already enough that one went to you and Dad's old town looking for clues. This dude is either real stupid or he has another plan in place." David shook his head in disgust. He couldn't believe someone would treat Daleigh like that. It was okay though. He was going to love her through this and after it. David and Maxine walked back downstairs and out to the back patio where everyone else had gathered. They wanted to give Daleigh as much peace and quiet as possible. Plus Dr. Shelby wanted to share some things the family could do to help Daleigh.

"Daleigh's mental and emotional health has been broken again. She can recover, but she's going to struggle, unfortunately. She's to need all hands on deck for this, including me. My house is nearby, so I can check in constantly. I will start having Daleigh's sessions here, as it will keep her from having to leave and anyone from taking a chance to hurt her." Dr. Shelby stated. Daleigh's safety was hinged on a lot. Everyone nodded in agreement with the plan. While they were outside talking, something was going on inside the house.

Retwist

Chaison quietly walked up the steps. He had been watching and following Daleigh for months. Jackson had been keeping him up to date on what was going on. Jackson didn't inherit the purple eyes his sister had. So no one knew who he really was. He knew exactly what was going on, so he knew how to move incognito. The last thing Jackson wanted was to be caught up in this whirlwind of mess. He felt Chaison should just leave Daleigh alone and let her hide out. But Chaison was concerned about what Maison could do to both of his kids. He may not have loved them, but he wouldn't let his twin hurt them either He felt he owed them that considering what had happened to their mom.

Chaison reached the room that Daleigh was sleeping in. He stood over her for a few minutes, deciding if he wanted to take the chance to remove her, or if he wanted to wait a few more days. He stared at her, remembering what Michelle looked like. Daleigh had a lot of her features. He hated Maison all over again. But he calmed himself so he could think rationally. Chaison had put in too much work getting this close. He figured Maison or Marcus might have figured him out by now. Chaison decided to wait until things were more stable before he made his move with Daleigh.

Marcus had arrived in Chiva very angry. He still hadn't heard from Chaison or Maison, and he was getting frustrated not being in the loop. He needed to know what was going on so he could make his next move.

Marcus got out of his car and walked into the little convenience store on the outskirts of the town to grab some sunflower seeds, a cold soda, and to find out some information. Chiva wasn't very big like Asdele wasn't. It only had a population of about 800 people. This was going to be easy and hard at the same time.

"Whattup man?" Marcus asked the cashier. She looked him up and down in disgust, wanting him out of her store.

"Nothin' much. Will that be all for you?" The cashier asked politely.

"I was wondering if you heard of a girl named Daleigh? Or have you seen a girl with purple eyes around?" Marcus wasn't liking how he was being treated. He glanced at the video monitor, then around the store to make sure no one else was there. He grabbed the young woman, pulling her almost over the counter. "Don't play with me, little girl. I want answers now before you get a taste of some bitter medicine."

"I-I-I don't know anyone by that name nor anybody with that eye color. I heard about some twins like that, but they're long gone from here. Please please, don't hurt me!!" The young woman was about to become hysterical, and Marcus couldn't have that. He slapped her so hard it knocked her unconscious. He laid her on the counter, took the drive in the recording system, grabbed his food and drink, and walked out of the store. He had also grabbed the keys to lock the door behind him. The store's location allowed for Marcus to be hidden, and the girl to probably wake up before anyone showed up needing anything. He threw the keys in the trash, ripped apart the drive, then tossed it in the trash also. Good luck with all that.

Marcus jumped in his car, popping sunflower seeds into his mouth. He was trying to figure out where to go next to get some help. He remember Maison mentioning one of the women he had been with in this city. Marcus just needed to remember her last name. All of a sudden, he remembered. Her last name was Dobson. But Marcus couldn't remember where the Dobsons stayed. He drove into the town, hoping to run into someone who could help him. He didn't want to see any police though. Marcus was trying to be as inconspicuous as possible. So far, it was working. He soon pulled up to a McDonald's. He ordered a burger and fries. He carried the soda he had purchased at the convenience store. Marcus sat off to the side of some old men chatting over coffee.

"Young David Dobson got a girl he likes," one of the old men stated.

"Well, who is she? Where did she come from? I heard she just popped up out the blue. Pretty girl though. I also heard her eyes are the same color as those evil twins Maison and Chaison. I'm glad they got run out of this town," another old man answered.

"Do you all know where she went?" Marcus tried to avoid being noticed, but his information and curiosity got the best of him.

"I don't rightly know," old man number 2 answered. I just know David'nem live over in Asdele. You know that about a 6-hour drive here right?" Old man number 2 was becoming quite curious, paying better attention to Marcus.

"Yes, I'm aware." Marcuse was fighting for his life to keep the sarcasm out of his voice so he could draw the rest of the information he needed. He wasn't going back to Maison and Chaison without either Daleigh or at least her whereabouts.

The old men chuckled. "What you so wound up about? She ain't all that important. She's just a pretty girl with eyes that ain't normal. Why would you want that?"

"Because she's my girlfriend. She went on a trip but she didn't tell me where she was going. It was a surprise trip, and I was supposed to join her. It just seems she forgot to give me the information for the hotel she was in." Marcus tried to make his voice sound as pitiful as possible. Unfortunately, he had to use the same tactics that he hated women using. But if it did the job, he would suck it up. He would deal with those old men last.

"Do you got a GPS or whatever them little digital maps on your phone is?" Old man number 3 spoke up.

"Yes, I have a GPS," Marcus answered, feeling rage starting to boil. It felt like the men were intentionally pulling his strings and not giving him information. "You have 30 seconds to explain to me where Daleigh is or I promise you won't walk out this McDonald's on your own two feet."

The men began getting nervous. One of them was remembering who Maison and Chasion were and how they had almost torn the small town to shreds. He realized who was standing in front of him. Marcus realized his recognition, and with his cold eyes, dared the man to speak. The old man quickly left the building and got in his car. The other two old men watched in confusion at what was happening. They were becoming scared themselves, especially when Marcus focused that gaze on them.

"Now, I'm going to ask for the last time. Where...is....Daleigh?!!"

CHAISON FELT HE WAS being followed. He rounded the corner, paused then hurriedly turned back around. Maison almost walked right into him.

"Really dude? Why are you following me?" Chaison said angrily.

"You know something. I know you do. Why would you even come here? There's nobody here." Maison said, squaring up with his brother.

"I have a contact here. He's got some information for me on finding Daleigh. You do want to find her right? Or do you not care about the mess your boy created? Why aren't you following him? Hasn't he ruined everything? Marcus is the reason why we got kicked out of Chiva. He's why we can't even go back. Like, bro, get rid of that dude. He's going to get us caught. We've been avoiding the police for the last 20 years. Marcus is insane bro." Chaison begged. What he didn't realize was that Maison was the craziest one. He would knock off his own brother if it meant getting Daleigh back in his hands. He still needed to deal with Marcus for losing her. And he knew just how he would do it. Chaison looked at his brother, a little fearful. He needed to get to Daleigh first. It was going to be hard though now that Maison was there.

"I need to get in touch with my contact. I think there's some information that we're missing." Chaison hurried away from Maison and phoned Jackson. He needed to get to Daleigh before the next day, otherwise he wouldn't be able to stop Maison.

Maison didn't know what was going on, but he knew his brother had a lead. He had watched him go into a house the day before. Maison had a feeling that either that's where Daleigh was, or someone who knew where she was. Right when he was about to interrogate his twin, his phone rang. Marcus was on the screen.

"Get to the point. I don't feel like talking." Maison answered in a cold voice, watching his brother walk away. He was getting tired of Chaison and Marcus. Both were incompetent.

Marcus answered quickly, "I found Daleigh. She's in a town called Asdele. No one knows who she's staying with though."

Marcus smiled his sly smile, "I know. Chaison is here. He says he's following a lead, but I don't believe him. How long will it take you to get here?"

Marcus glanced at the time left on the GPS. He had jumped in his truck and hit the road as soon as he had finished with the old men. "It'll take me bout an hour and a half to get there," Maison grunted in agreement and told Marcus to meet him at the Asdele Walmart. He was about to shake things up a bit. Daleigh needed to understand that you don't get to leave once one of them gets hold of you. Maison watched Chaison drive down the road, then jumped on his motorcycle to follow, this time from far enough so Chaison wouldn't notice. He mentally rubbed his hands together. He was going to love this.

DALEIGH WALKED OUT of the rec center having completed her last day of classes. Almost 6 months had passed since she moved to Asdele. Dr. Shelby was still checking on her from time to time to ensure she was on par with home treatment. Daleigh officially had her certificate. She and David were going to look at some shop spaces so Daliegh could open her own event planning office. She was content with David by her side. He didn't rush things. He loved her through the nights when she screamed, cried, and even shut down. He always encouraged her to take whatever time she needed to heal and cope. The road ahead for Daleigh and David was a long one yet they were traveling it together, supporting one another.

"Well hello there." A man stepped in front of Daleigh before she could open her car door. Oddly, the man had the same shade of purple eye she did. Daleigh began to shake uncontrollably. She couldn't find her voice to scream. She stared at the man in disbelief.

"I'm just here to protect you. My name is Chaison. I'm your dad," Chaison spoke quickly. He knew from doing several days of surveillance that a lot of days Daleigh would arrive at and leave the rec center alone. Most days either Janice or David were with her. The days changed often, so it was hard to pick up on the right days. Today was the perfect opportunity for Chaison to fix the problem.

"Wh-What do you want with me?" Daleigh asked, her voice trembling as violently as her body.

Chaison smiled at Daleigh. This was his daughter. The product of one night with the only woman he would ever love. "I'm here to take you to safety. Why don't you come with me and I'll get you out of here." Chaison offered. Just when Daleigh took a curious step forward, the sound of a motorcycle interrupted them. Maison pulled up just in time.

"Well hello there daughter. I see you've met your uncle. I've got a surprise for you," Maison said, the coldness of his voice causing Daleigh to stop shivering and question Maison's meaning. Suddenly, Marcus pulls up in his truck. Daleigh tries to run in the opposite direction. The problem is Jackson is standing on that end, blocking the escape.

"Jackson!! I thought you were helping me. Why are you helping them? You're supposed to be a police officer, upholding the law." Daleigh said in confusion. She didn't know what was going on. All she knew was that she needed to run. The sooner the better.

"Don't think about running Baby Girl," Marcus smirked. He had planned to ensure Daleigh would never run away again. Not only would he keep her locked from the world, but he was to discipline her and make her obey.

Daleigh reached for her phone in her purse. Usually, it was in her pocket, but she had to finish all the designs and papers from her event planning class. Now she wished she had stuck the phone in her pocket. Daliegh was always looking around to see if anyone was willing to help her. Chaison shook his head, then looked Daleigh right in the eerily similar eyes.

"There's nowhere to go. Just come with us and we won't hurt anyone. Jackson knows all the people here." Chaison had decided to change his strategy with Daliegh. As she was staring at him, Jackson moved in behind Daleigh, bound her hands and feet, and placed a pillowcase over her head. Daleigh tried to struggle, but it was to no avail. Jackson tossed her in the back of his squad car.

"Where do you want me to take her?" he asked.

"We're headed back to Chiva," Maison answered. It was time to go back to the beginning. As the men started to leave with Daleigh, Dr. Shelby ran out of the rec center. Something had felt off, so she went to check it out. Sure enough, Daleigh was being kidnapped. Dr. Shebly knew who was behind it before she even saw their faces. It had been a long time since she had seen them. Dr. Shelby was hoping to never have to deal with them again. Yet here they were. She smiled with vengeance. Dr. Shelby was going to get Maison, Chaison, and Marcus. She called

Jackson because he could get the word of Daleigh's kidnapping out fast. She held a secret that couldn't be out too soon.

DALEIGH'S EYES OPENED in the dimly lit room. Jackson pulled the pillowcase off her head. She was genuinely confused. Daleigh wanted to ask questions, but she refused to be lied to or manipulated. Maison and Chaison were arguing in a corner, which was making Marcus' head hurt. He was tired. He just wanted to take Daleigh and leave.

"Bruh, I don't care what you say. I'm going to keep her for myself." Chaison said. He and Maison had finally calmed down. Maison was still on high alert and was waiting for Chaison to make a move. He was learning over time that his identical twin was the complete opposite of him. There would be no going back on this one.

"I'm not going to tell you again. She's my daughter, a gift to Marcus for helping us in Chiva." Maison was on the verge of fighting again. He could do whatever he wanted to with Daleigh. Who was big and bad enough to stop him? Nobody. Her mother was dead. There was no other family other than his twin. Chaison was weak in Maison's eyes. If he was strong, he never would have let Maison take Michelle from him. Stupid idiot.

"What if I told you she wasn't your daughter?" Chaison had Maison baited. Maison looked straight into the identical eyes that he had staring into his face. Chaison had a knowing smirk. He was about to rip Maison's life to shreds. He was tired of his brother treating him like a lap dog. Things ended today. Now whether anyone was going to walk away from this was yet to be seen.

"She isn't your daughter, Maison!" Dr. Shelby walked into the room. The men hadn't paid attention to being followed. Dr. Shelby followed them to Maison and Chaison's family home in Chiva. It was on the outskirts of the town, tucked away on a dirt road. There were plenty of trees that surrounded it. If you didn't pay attention and know where you were going, you could miss the house. It had been empty for almost 20 years, the time when the twins had finally moved on to find trouble somewhere else. Marcus had left to drive trucks.

Maison turned around in shock. Where had this woman come from? And why did she look familiar? Maison cocked his head in interest at the new development. He had a feeling something unexpected was about to happen. All the alarms in his head were going off. Chaison had shock on his face. Dr. Shelby felt familiar to him also. Marcus looked like he was ready to run out of the room. The only calm one was Jackson, which was eerie. It almost seemed as if he was expecting what was happening and about to happen.

"Daleigh is Chaison's daughter. And Jackson is her twin." Dr. Shelby glanced around the room, taking in every reaction. Jackson's face was stoic. He knew that Chaison was his father. He didn't know that Daliegh was his twin. Chaison looked as if he was about to pass out. Maison had changed the atmosphere in the room. It felt like a freezer had been turned on. His face was full of fury. Marcus was looking around in confusion. Wasn't the reason Maison gave him Daleigh because she was his daughter? If she wasn't, then that meant that he was going to have to deal with Chaison. Marcus knew Maison was insane. Chaison didn't give those kinds of vibes. Yet, the saying goes the quiet one is usually the one you want to watch.

"How?! How do you know?!" Daleigh screamed, confused. She had a twin and now knew who her father was.

"Because I am your mother," Dr. Shelby said quietly. "My name is Diana Shelby. My real name is Michelle Dean." She turned to Maison. "You thought you killed me, leaving me in that ditch. We made everyone think I was dead. I lived Maison. Your plan backfired. Your torture of your brother stops today!!"

Chaison placed himself between Maison and Michelle. While Michelle was talking, Maison had started walking toward her, aiming to really finish her since the first time failed. Chaison wasn't about to lose the love of his life a second time. She had given him two children. He would protect them and her with his life.

"You better start explaining," Maison demanded.

"I was pregnant with twins. It's why I never wanted you to go with me to the doctor's appointments. When it was time for them to be born, I wouldn't allow you in the OR. I had someone take Jackson. I only kept Jaida, well, Daleigh. What I didn't expect was you to kill me out, then kidnap my daughter. You left me in that ditch to die. You hit me with the car because Chaison came to check on me. Do you hate him that much, Maison? I was with you so you wouldn't hurt him. You told me if I became your girl, you would leave him alone. You beat me on purpose. You used me to play games with Chaison's head. Are you satisfied? You still didn't win!!" Michelle was livid.

"So...that's how it is. All of you played in my face huh? I promise I'm going to get all of you back. Especially you Chaison. I'm your twin. Your brother. You would choose this chick over me? We have been together for a lifetime." Maison was in shock. His twin, his woman, and apparently the man he thought was on his side but was really his nephew all betrayed him. Maison started forming his payback plan. While he wasn't paying attention, Jackson had set Daleigh free. He walked up to Maison and placed him in handcuffs. Marcus tried to run, but Chaison didn't let him get far. At that moment, the police came into the room, followed by Janice, James, and David. Janice made a beeline to Daleigh, checking to make sure she wasn't hurt in any way. David waited until his aunt was done, then he did his own check.

"I'm fine. Where's my mom and dad?" Daleigh asked, searching the room for Chaison and Michelle.

"They're gone," Jackson answered. He pulled Daleigh into a hug. "I had them leave while the police were dealing with Maison and Marcus. They're not coming back."

Daleigh began to sob. She had just met her parents, and they had to leave her. She felt abandoned all over again. Her heart was going to have to heal all over again.

"Wait....Jackson, aren't you David's cousin? What does that make me to him?!" Daleigh asked.

"He's my cousin through adoption. He's not my biological cousin." Jackson answered quickly. He knew how David felt about Daleigh, and the last thing he wanted was something not important to interfere with that.

"Ok!! Let's go home!!" Janice clapped her hands.

Jackson explained everything on the way back to Asdele. How Michelle had him taken away after being born to protect him. That Daleigh was his twin. Them finding out that Chaison is their father, not Maison. No one was sure what would happen now that Michelle was still alive. Maison and Marcus were headed to jail, but how long would those bars hold them? They would just have to wait and see.

Chaison looked at Michelle. His heart was full. He never thought he could love. Michelle had shown him how. When Maison had taken her, Chaison thought that it was only because he liked Michelle. He never thought it was to continually hurt and abuse him with it. It was ok though. He was going to spend the rest of his life with Michelle, the way it should have been many years before. He smiled at her and he pressed the gas a little harder, pushing the car to go faster down the highway, and further away from Chiva and Asdele.

Locced and Loaded

Daleigh and David arrived at David's parent's house for Thanksgiving. Dalegh had been planning David's friend's wedding. She had chosen the colors, the wedding dress, and all the other details. David had planned things on the groom's side, stating that his friend was overseas and couldn't do it himself. David's family, all 25 of them, were gathered at the house. Maxine was in the kitchen with her sisters and mother, making sure the food was cooked and that the dishes that were bought were warm. Dennis was moving things around in the yard for the coming children.

Daleigh walked to the back door, watching David and Dennis clear the yard. Her heart was so whole. She never imagined in 2 years that she would be meeting and marrying a man who could love her despite her brokenness. Marcus had almost shattered her into a shell of a person. Despite all the therapy and prayer, she could never understand how someone could be so vicious and uncaring. How could someone destroy a person's heart and life without a second thought? Marcus was going to rot in prison, though. And he deserved it. The lies, manipulation, and abuse were finally over. She could breathe, and it felt so good. When Daleigh arrived in Atley, her life was in shambles. Now, she was at a level of healing she didn't know she could achieve.

"What are you thinking about, beautiful? Your forehead will get bigger if you keep wrinkling it like that." David said jokingly.

"I'm thinking about how amazing healing has been and putting the finishing touches on this wedding for your friend. By the way, when are he and the bride coming so I can make sure they're happy with everything?" Daleigh said.

"Ummm...later. Why don't you help Mom in the kitchen? My aunts just pulled up." David said quickly and dashed back out the door. He just stepped in. Something was going on; Daleigh just couldn't figure out what. David had been acting strange since he asked her to be a wedding planner for his friend Jarvis. The thing is, Daleigh had never met Jarvis. The planning was almost like winging it. She had to choose everything for the bridal party and wedding colors. Something was up, and she intended to find out by the end of Thanksgiving dinner.

David realized he had almost got caught by Daleigh. He could tell she was curious about the wedding planning and why she chose instead of the supposed bride and groom. He had devised this plan last Christmas when he knew he wanted to spend the rest of his life with Daleigh. David had fallen in love with Daleigh long before he told her, but he wanted there to be no pressure on her healing process. He hated how Marcus had broken her but was proud of how Daleigh had put herself back together. To him, she deserved all the love in the world and more. He was also proud of the way she dealt with her parents. That was a long road to be still traveled. David would ensure Jason and Casey never interfered in Daleigh's life again. They almost cost her her life. He would make sure she was protected at all costs. David smiled to himself as he thought about the surprise in his pocket. It was about to be a crazy holiday, and he would love every minute.

Daleigh glanced out the window to check on David as she helped Maxine and her sisters Cindy and Sheila finish preparing the food. She saw the smile on his face, and it made her heart smile. David had become everything she had waited for. She couldn't wait until the day when they could take their relationship to the level of marriage. Until that day, she would continue healing and growing into the woman she needed to be and the wife she wanted to be. Soon, everyone was called into the dining. The table was heavy with a 25 lb turkey, greens (turnip, collard, and mustard), homemade cornbread, mashed potatoes, chicken and turkey dressing, homemade cranberry sauce, baked chicken, rice, gravy, and candied yams. There was another smaller table with caramel apple pie, sweet potato pie, different kinds of pound cake, and a pecan pit. There were about 25 people in all in the beautiful Southwestern room. The upper ceiling was made of wood burnt in certain spots to look smoked. The walls were a sage green color, and there was a long cedar table that could seat about 30 people. The chairs were made of a light oak. The family stood around the table, joining hands. Maxine asked Dannis to pray over the food and family.

"Everyone bow your heads. Dear Heavenly Father, we thank You for another chance to be gathered together here as a family. Thank You for bringing everyone here safely. Thank You for the new additions to our family...especially my daughter-in-law."

Daleigh's head popped up as she squeezed David's hand. What daughter-in-law? Daleigh felt David release her hand. She turned toward him to see he had gotten down on one knee. She could see his nervousness and tears. Her whole body began shaking.

"Daleigh, you have been the sunshine in my life. You have encouraged me to improve even when your life was in shambles. I don't want to be another day without you. I want to help you keep growing and healing. I want to walk with you through everything. Will you marry me?" David said, his voice trembling.

"Yes!!" Daleigh didn't realize her voice was so high that she startled herself. David placed the emerald and diamond ring on her finger, then took her into his arms. He buried his head in her neck as she wet his with her tears. Her body was shaking even harder as her tears turned into sobs. This was indeed something to be thankful for. Daleigh was brought back to reality when family members started congratulating the couple.

"So when do we start planning?" Maxine asked, tears streaming down her face while she smiled in joy.

"On Saturday," David answered, glancing over at Daleigh.

"Say what now?!! How are we going to get married on Saturday? Isn't that your friend's wedding date?" Suddenly, things began to click in Daleigh's head. The dress. The colors. The theme. The cake. The bridesmaid's dresses her friends had modeled for her. You are taking her to choose a ring and getting her ring size. David had Daleigh planning her wedding without her knowledge. "You think you're slick, don't you?"

"No. I just wanted to surprise you." David said sheepishly, wondering what Daleigh would do to him for lying. He prayed she wouldn't hold it against him too long for tricking her. He loved her so much and wanted the day to be unique. David could tell he would pay the price for lying for a long time.

"I'm still going to marry you on Saturday. You just better watch your back between then and now," Daleigh said with a small smile.

Dennis got everyone's attention with the whistle of his lips. "Ok, family!! Let's eat before the food gets cold. I think that prayer doesn't even need to be continued." He grabbed the knife so he could begin cutting the turkey. He was so proud of David. Daleigh was an amazing young woman who had overcome almost losing her life. God allowed David to find her and be there for her through all of it. Dennis and Maxine were excited about getting a daughter. They had no other children besides David, and Daleigh was the perfect match for him. He glanced over at his wife, smiling from ear to tear. Maxine helped David plan the surprise wedding behind the scenes. Daleigh only knew so much until today because of the stories. David was glad everything was out in the open because lying to Daleigh was eating all of them up. Their family helped prepare the catering and decorations.

Daleigh looked around the table after she sat next to David and prepared her plate. Her heart was beating so fast that she was having a hard time eating. She was engaged to such a fantastic man and about to become part of a great and loving family. Dennis and Maxine always showed her how a true mother and father should treat their child. Both of their families loved her and had, in so many words, adopted her. She was delighted thinking of the love she had received from them. Her world was finally right. The family finished dinner and then gathered in the yard so the children could play. There was a TV set up so the holiday football and basketball games could be watched. The children ran around the yard, jumping in the bouncing houses, playing with the balls, and chasing each other.

"This is what love and family feel like," Daleigh thought, glancing over at David. She blushed as she realized David had been watching her. He smiled at her, mouthing "I love you" to her. Daleigh began smiling back.

"Awwww!!! Look at the babies all smiley and stuff!!" Aunt Janice said loudly enough for the whole neighborhood to hear.

"Really, Auntie? Really?!" Daleigh and David said at the same time.

"Oh, am I embarrassing y'all? Wait until Saturday. I'm gone show yall embarrassing!!" Aunt Janice huffed.

"Sis!! Why can't you act right for one?" Dennis muttered to his sister. "James, come get your wife, man!! She actin' up again, and ain't nobody got time for that."

James pulled Janice into a hug. "Man, don't act like that to your sister. You know she loves you and David like he was her own. Daleigh has already stolen her heart. They are like our kids."

Knowing the situation for James and Janice, Dennis just shook his head and let it go. He loved his sister, especially knowing that her story resembled Daleigh's. Janice's ex-boyfriend had beaten her so severely that he damaged her uterus. She was never able to have children. Thankfully, James loved her through it all. Dennis was glad his sister had the love and support, and David loved Daleigh the same way.

Dennis didn't know if David and Daleigh could have kids yet, but only time would tell.

"Well, is everyone ready for Saturday?" Maxine asked the table. All cousins nodded, the aunts squealed their delight, and all the uncles nodded and smiled. This would be the biggest wedding the family had ever been a part of.

"Daleigh, how are you feeling, babe?" David asked/

"I'm freakin out!! Like, you did this, baby. My heart is overflowing. Come on Saturday!! I've planned our epic day. I promise there will be no dry eyes. And you, sir, will be able to kiss me finally!!" Daeigh's excitement could hardly be contained.

Saturday arrived bright and beautiful. The sun was out, and the air was cool, but the wind didn't blow. The leaves were the perfect shades of brown, orange, and red, contrasting the white, lavender, and blue outside the church. Balloons and flowers were decorating the stairs and outer edges of the church.

The white limousine pulled up. Daleigh, her friends, and David's cousins stepped out, all 9 of them. There was excitement in the air, jumping from person to person. Daleigh and the ladies headed into the church. They talked about how the weather was perfect for such a day. They each prepared for hair and makeup. The dresses were already in the room on the hangars. The bridesmaids' dresses were an array of lavender, royal blue, and white. They were off-shoulder, white with a blue and lavender sash. The maid of honor dress was a deep purple with a blue and white sash. The dress was off-shoulder. The wedding dress was white, with a lavender sash and train and a lavender veil. The shoes were blue and white. Daleigh had blue and white flowers sewn into the veil. She touched her dress, caressing it in awe of its beauty and ready to put it on.

All the ladies went to the chairs in the room and started talking to the hair and makeup stylists. Each woman had a particular style that she wanted her hair in. Daleigh's hair was colored a rich brown, and her locs were placed in rollers to produce pretty curls. The other ladies had cascade curls. They all dressed, then helped Daleigh dress. Maxine came in in her lavender mother-of-the-groom dress and hugged Daleigh. Both had tears running down their faces. She then called all the women to gather around her. They circled Daleigh. Maxine placed her hands on Daleigh's shoulders and began to pray. By the time the prayer was over, not one eye was dry.

David, Dennis, and the other men arrived about 30 minutes after the women did. They all walked into the back of the church, where they would get dressed. The groomsmen's suits were dark blue, with white cummerbunds and lavender bowties. David's suit was white, with a blue bowtie and lavender cummerbund. All the men's shoes were white. David couldn't be still. His excitement was starting to rub off on everyone else in the room. Dennis was trying to get him to calm down, yet he was getting excited. His only child was getting married and starting his own family. James called for all the men to gather around David, and Dennis led them in prayer. David went from nervous excitement to just excitement. His pounding heart began to slow down. He looked at his father as he finished the prayer. Their eyes locked, and Dennis nodded knowingly at David. His son was ready to see his bride.

David and his groomsmen stood at the front of the church. David was facing the pastor as he was not allowed to look back at the door. The church smelled of lavender, roses, and jasmine, as those flowers were connected and hanging around the whole church. There were lavender, white, and blue ribbons around the church. The music started, and David could hear the door open to let the bridesmaids and maid of honor walk in. As the song finished, the door closed again. David inhaled sharply. His queen was getting ready to walk in. The door opened, and tears began to run down David's face. He could hear Daleigh crying.

Daleigh took a deep breath before the doors opened. She saw David's back and couldn't control her sobs anymore. She began to inhale and exhale slowly. Daleigh needed to calm down so she could call David's name and he could face her. She stopped crying long enough to say "David!!". He turned around and broke down even more. He couldn't believe how beautiful Daliegh looked. She couldn't believe how handsome David was in his suit. She wanted to run to him, but she walked towards him. David stared in awe as Daleigh moved in his direction in time with the music playing. He could move nothing but his eyes. When she arrived in front of him, he grabbed her and pulled her close. It felt like no one else was in the church. When David finally let Daleigh go so they could face the pastor, not one person had a dry eye. The pastor had to clear his throat a few times before he began.

"Dearly beloved, we are gathered here today to celebrate the union of David and Daleigh. If anyone believes they should not be married, speak now or forever hold your peace."

David, Daleigh, the bridesmaids, and the groomsmen stared daggers around the room. No one had better say anything. The whole wedding party was ready to throw hands if necessary. Everyone sat awkwardly for a few seconds, and then the pastor continued.

"David, your vows."

"Daleigh, you mean everything to me. The day I met you, I knew you would change my life. I just didn't know how. You have trusted me during the most challenging time in your life. You allowed me to hold your hand. You didn't depend on me to heal you, yet you let me love you while you were healing. You have supported and pushed me when I felt I didn't have enough to give. I'm so proud of you. You opened a business. You pushed through every bad thing that came your way. I love you. I'm glad I get to do the rest of my life with you. I, David Robson, take you, Daleigh Miller, as my lawfully wedded wife. To have and to hold. To love and to cherish. For richer and for poorer. In sickness and in health. Until death do us part. I promise to push you, love you, be beside you, cheer you on, and help you grow. I promise to be submitted to God and love you as God loves us. I love you, my queen." David stated firmly through his tears.

Daleigh stared into David's eyes. "David, I love you so much. You are the answer to a prayer that I never knew I prayed. Thank you for being there for me and loving me when I doubted anyone could. Thank you for giving me a family. Mom and Dad, thank you for treating me as your daughter. David, I take you as my husband. I promise to love and cherish you, To have and hold you. To submit to you and to follow you as you follow Christ. I promise to be a support and best friend. Til death do us part. You saw the hurt me and didn't try to heal me with your love. You loved me through my healing. When I wanted to push you away, you stood firm. You hugged me, screamed with me, and protected me when I was attacked. Thank you for choosing me. I love you, King."

The pastor led the church into prayer, placing his hands on David and Daleigh's heads as they knelt. Dennis and Maxine stood behind them with their hands on both of them. The church all had their hands stretched out toward the couple. The pastor then asked if the family, friends, and church would hold the couple accountable to their vows. After there was a loud agreement, several songs were performed. Daleigh and David exchanged rings, then the special moment of the day came.

"Are you ready for our first official ever kiss, Mrs. Dobson?" David quietly asked Daleigh.

"Yes, Mr. Dobson, I'm ready," Daleigh whispered. David lifted the veil from Daleigh's face, whispered, "I love you," and gently kissed her. Daleigh closed her eyes, savoring the moment. She was kissing her husband!! Everyone started clapping and cheering. Today was the first day of the rest of David and Daleigh's lives. They turned and then ran toward the back of the church. The doors opened, and they jumped into the waiting limo.

Don't miss out!

Visit the website below and you can sign up to receive emails whenever Candi Jones publishes a new book. There's no charge and no obligation.

https://books2read.com/r/B-A-VLJDB-LKEBF

BOOKS 2 READ

Connecting independent readers to independent writers.

Also by Candi Jones

Locceed and Loaded Ladies
Locced and Loaded Ladies: Daleigh's Journey

Standalone
Pretty Wings

Watch for more at https://www.candisthoughts.com.

About the Author

I am a mother, cook, daughter, and a Disabled Navy Veteran. Winning is my therapy. It is my distraction on bad days. It is also my strength on good days. I love writing because I can put my thoughts on paper, creating stories that touch the heart, mind, and Spirit. Read into you imagination.

Read more at https://www.candisthoughts.com.